Shi

Rafe the hunters and Sheila

ELLORA'S CAVE
ROMANTICA PUBLISHING

An Ellora's Cave Romantica Publication

www.ellorascave.com

The Hunters: Rafe and Sheila

ISBN # 1419952994
ALL RIGHTS RESERVED.
The Hunters: Rafe and Sheila Copyright© 2005 Shiloh Walker
Edited by: Pamela Campbell
Cover art by: Syneca

Electronic book Publication: May, 2005
Trade paperback Publication: November, 2005

Excerpt from *Ben and Shadoe* Copyright © Shiloh Walker, 2005

Warning:

The following material contains graphic sexual content meant for mature readers. *The Hunters: Rafe and Sheila* has been rated *E-rotic* by a minimum of three independent reviewers.

Ellora's Cave Publishing offers three levels of Romantica™ reading entertainment: S (S-ensuous), E (E-rotic), and X (X-treme).

S-ensuous love scenes are explicit and leave nothing to the imagination.

E-rotic love scenes are explicit, leave nothing to the imagination, and are high in volume per the overall word count. In addition, some E-rated titles might contain fantasy material that some readers find objectionable, such as bondage, submission, same sex encounters, forced seductions, etc. E-rated titles are the most graphic titles we carry; it is common, for instance, for an author to use words such as "fucking", "cock", "pussy", etc., within their work of literature.

X-treme titles differ from E-rated titles only in plot premise and storyline execution. Unlike E-rated titles, stories designated with the letter X tend to contain controversial subject matter not for the faint of heart.

Also by Shiloh Walker:

Rafe and Sheila

The Hunters

Trademarks Acknowledgement

The author acknowledges the trademarked status and trademark owners of the following wordmarks mentioned in this work of fiction:

Chevy BelAir: General Motors Corporation
Crown Vic: Ford Motor Company

Prologue

Sheila looked up from the table where she was helping Erika with her homework, watching as Rafe moved closer to the house. She couldn't see him yet, but she felt him. He was close.

Her body always seemed to cry out in agony when he left — and it rejoiced when he returned. Right now, she was clamoring for him and that was really very pathetic.

Absently, she listened as Erika worked her way through the advanced algebra problems. Inside her chest, her heart had picked up, pounding along at a steady forty beats a minute. Her skin felt hot and tight and she ached inside.

As he came through the door in silence, she smiled at him.

Her heart broke a little more when he ignored her, focusing his attention on Erika as he swung a chair around and straddled it, sitting down beside the princess of the house. Sheila held still for long moments as they spoke. She felt brittle, stung by yet another brush-off from him, and she was afraid that if she moved too suddenly, she just might shatter at his feet.

He rose a few minutes later, that thick, waving black hair tumbling into his dark Italian eyes, his olive complexion glowing. He had Hunted and fed before he'd returned home. She could smell the scent of another person on him as he moved past.

Her gaze lingered on his face as he gave her a brusque nod before he left the kitchen.

Tears burned her eyes as she lowered them, trying to focus on the book in front of her.

Erika whispered softly, "He likes you."

Sliding the girl a glance, she forced a smile and said, "Of course he does."

Erika rolled her eyes as she murmured, "I mean like *that*. The way you like him. He just doesn't like it."

Sheila wrapped an arm around Erika's shoulders and squeezed gently. "We've got to get this done…we got TV to watch," she said, changing the subject and guiding the girl's uncanny, insightful eyes back to her work.

* * * * *

Rafe scowled as Sheila left the house, head low, her steps slow. She had donned the dark, close-fitting clothes she wore when she Hunted and he couldn't keep his eyes away from the way the black fatigues stretched across that delightfully round ass.

He had missed her.

Gone three weeks to Excelsior, and all he could think about was her.

He had sensed her the moment he'd stepped back on Eli's lands and his blood had seemed to burn inside his veins. Hunger had throbbed in his cock, in his head, tightening his muscles. Seeing her, he had wanted nothing more than to sink to his knees in front of her and wrap his arms around her, burying his face between her full, rounded breasts.

She made him weak.

And he *hated* it.

So he had ignored what he wanted, ignored the hesitant smile in her eyes, keeping his attention focused on Erika, ignoring the pain he felt coming from her.

She knew the score, damn it. After giving Erika a slight smile, he had left the kitchen, his scowl deepening once he was out of their sight.

Now, a day later, he couldn't stop craving a taste of her. Sheila hadn't been in her rooms today—he had no idea where she had slept. And he refused to go looking for her.

Just after sunset, she had returned, her eyes hooded. The long sweep of her rose-colored skirt flowed down the length of her thighs, and a pretty sweater, shades darker than the skirt, gave color to her creamy complexion. Rafe watched her from the greatroom where the Hunters of Eli's enclave had gathered for the night. Watched as she sauntered in and dropped onto a couch between Mike and Jonathan. Lori was sitting in Jonathan's lap, so the two of them took up a little more room, meaning that Sheila had to sit closer to Mike than Rafe could stand. Studiously, she ignored the looks he slid her, staring at Eli with intent, focused eyes.

That had sliced. Deep.

Mike's dark gray eyes slid to Rafe as Sheila sat there. Rafe scowled, jerking his gaze away from the Inherent, knowing his anger was naked for all to see.

When the meeting ended she left for her night of patrol with her shoulders slumped and her eyes on the ground. Damn it. The southern belle looked about as happy as he felt.

In his hands, he held a short sword, polishing a surface that really didn't need it. The blade all but glowed in the dim light, reflecting his face back at him as he tore his eyes from Sheila's form, forcing himself to look at the sword as he ran the cloth up and down.

But barely a moment passed before he lifted his gaze again, searching for Sheila once more. She was gone from sight.

Out Hunting.

Walking away from him…

Hunger, pain, guilt, need—they all ran together and wrapped a tight fist around his heart. Laying the sword aside, he spun away from the window to pace the floor.

She *knew*. He'd warned her from the beginning that he wasn't the man for a relationship. Not that she ever asked for anything. But he saw the disappointment in her eyes every time he pulled back. Sheila wanted more. Hell, that was what she was made for. And he couldn't give it to her.

But he'd be damned if he'd let her walk away.

Seeing her warmed something inside him that he thought had died long ago. Any man who so much as looked at her had him ready to kill.

He stalked into her rooms, ignoring his own as he dropped down on her bed and closed his eyes. Her scent was everywhere—her touch all over the place. Wrapped in it, he let it soothe the ache in his gut while he waited.

* * * * *

Sheila came to an abrupt halt just inside her door.

Rafe lay on the bed, his long, lean limbs sprawled sexily, the mellow gold of his skin gleaming against the white eyelet comforter. He wore jeans. Just jeans.

Her heart leaped into her throat, dancing a jig as his eyes opened.

A light dusting of hair trailed down the center of his chest, thickening into a darker line that disappeared under the waistband of his jeans. In the dim light, he stared at her from hooded eyes, his mouth curved in just the slightest of smiles.

The muscles in his belly worked as he sat up slowly, his eyes dark, all but glowing with hunger.

Her own hunger was a pulsing thing in her belly, throbbing and hot. The urge to leap atop him and kiss him senseless rose, but she beat it down.

Two days. He'd been back two bloody days, and he hadn't said so much as a word to her. But now, he was in here waiting for her, and she knew damned well why. Not to talk to her, not to hold her or tell her that he'd missed her.

Just to fuck her. His cock strained under the sturdy denim cloth and she could hear his heartbeat picking up as he stared at her.

Nothing more. She loved him, with every fiber of her being and she was nothing more than a way for him to slake his hunger.

Sheila wasn't doing this anymore. He ignored her, except when he wanted to fuck her. And she just couldn't take it anymore.

"Get out, Rafe," she said quietly, walking away from the bed, sitting down on the chair in front of her vanity, her fingers going to the band that held her braid together.

"Rough night, Belle?"

His voice, as always, made her shiver. Sliding him a blank glance, she lifted one shoulder and said, "No. The night went fine. Get out."

In the mirror, she could see him as he rose. That vampires didn't cast a reflection was a lie. They all had one. And his was moving closer to her. Her hands fell away as he took the thick cable of her braid in his hands, slowly unwinding it, combing through the wavy locks, taking an inordinate amount of time doing so, smoothing it down along her shoulders and back, stroking down the locks that spilled over the upper mounds of her breasts.

As the flats of his hands brushed against her nipples, Sheila bit back the whimper that rose in her throat. Throwing off his hands, she stood up and moved away, walking to her closet and kneeling down to unlace her boots. "How many times do I have to tell you to get out, Rafe?" she asked quietly.

For a long while, he was silent, and when she raised her head to look at him, a shiver raced down her spine at the intent, hungry look in his eyes. "You kicking me out, Belle?" he asked gruffly.

"I don't want you in here." Her voice shook as she said it, but it was nothing more than the truth.

Her heart was breaking. It shattered into tiny pieces every time he brushed her off, every time he rose from the bed after fucking her and refused to stay, refused to hold her close as the sun rose in the sky. She couldn't do this anymore.

"What exactly are you saying, Sheila?"

Swallowing, she looked up from her crouched position and said quietly, "It's over, Rafe. You kept telling me you could only give me so much. Well, I don't want it anymore. Not if I never get anything else from you. Now get *out*."

A cold look entered his eyes and he crossed to her, kneeling in front of her. As his hand cupped the back of her neck, Sheila braced herself, seeing the naked fury in his eyes, the disbelief… For a second, she thought she saw a flicker of pain. But this was Rafe. He didn't give a damn about her, not beyond sex.

"You expect me to believe you don't want me anymore?" he asked, drawing her closer as he spoke. "Don't want this?"

Sheila clenched her jaw as he slanted his mouth across hers, his tongue — that hot sinful tongue — seeking entrance to her closed lips. His hand came up when she refused to admit him, cupping her jaw, pressing down just there until her mouth opened unwillingly.

As he pushed his tongue inside her mouth, she bit him, trying to jerk away. "Damn it, Rafe, stop it!" she rasped, arching her neck away from him.

"You want me, Sheila. You know it…I can smell the cream in your pussy, the fire in your blood. You want me — but you think you can kick me out?" he growled.

She flattened her hands against his chest, shoving with all her might, but he didn't budge. More than a hundred years older than she was, Rafe was a dominant vampire, and there was no way she could move him if he didn't want to be moved.

"Stop it, Rafe," she whimpered. Heat sizzled through her veins. He hadn't lied. She did want him. Lightning streaks of pleasure suffused her pussy as he ground himself against her and her body ached for his touch.

But she'd made up her mind. Damn it, it was over. With a tiny scream of rage, she reached up and yanked on his hair—hard—and as his hands loosened on her, she rolled away from him, coming to her feet and crossing the room as he rose and turned to glare at her.

"What, Sheila? You in the mood to play rough?" he drawled.

Crossing her arms over her chest, she hugged herself. She shook her head, staring at him as tears started to well in her eyes. "I want you to leave, Rafe," she whispered thickly. Blinking away the tears, she glared at him as he continued to stand there, staring at her. "*Leave!*"

Rafe knew he was being an ass. He couldn't stop it. Damn it, she wasn't going to do this. He crossed to her, cornering her against the wall, planting his hands on either side of her as she tried to sidle away. Lowering his head, he raked his teeth along her neck, catching her hands and pinning them beside her head when she tried to shove him away.

"Easy, Belle," he whispered. "I'm sorry...I know I'm a jerk. I just want you too much. I hate it. Don't kick me out."

His heart clenched in his chest as she turned her face aside and he saw a tear trickle down her cheek.

"Rafe, just leave me alone, please."

Covering her trembling mouth with his, he told himself this had to stop. He couldn't keep putting that pain in her eyes. All he wanted now was to kiss it away.

He crushed her body against his, wrapping his arms around her as he brought her wrists behind her, pinning them at the small of her back. He rocked his cock against the softness of her belly, breathing in the soft scent of her body.

"Just let me…" he murmured.

Sheila whispered again, "Rafe, don't. Just leave me alone."

A cool wind passed through the room, awareness trickling down his spine as the sincerity of her words finally hit home. As he lifted his head, he grew aware of eyes on him. Staring down at her, he realized that she wouldn't accept him. If he took her now, it would be rape.

"Leave her alone, Rafe," a soft, faintly accented voice stated.

"Eli, this isn't your concern," he said, slowly releasing Sheila, shame burning hot in his belly as he flicked a glance at his Master before stepping back from Sheila.

"Well, unfortunately, that is where you are wrong," Eli countered, his voice flat and cold. "This is my land, my territory. Sheila is one of my people and taking care of her is definitely my concern."

Rafe watched as Sheila slid to the ground, her cheeks bright pink with shame, tears rolling steadily down her face. He turned and glared at Eli. "I wouldn't hurt her," he snarled.

Behind Eli, the werewolf Jonathan stood, his face grim, eyes swirling. Rage flowed off of Jonathan in waves and suddenly, Rafe realized how close he had come to doing just that.

That close…to taking her, whether she wanted him or not.

Closing his eyes, he forced himself to take a deep breath, trying to still the hunger inside him. Finally his eyes opened and he stared at Eli with an unreadable expression.

"I wouldn't have hurt her, Eli," he said quietly.

From the corner of his eye, he watched as Sheila flinched at his words and he felt sick at his stomach.

Eli was silent.

It was Jonathan who spoke up, his voice rough and low, angry. "Rafe, you've already hurt her. Can't you see that?"

Lifting his head, he stared at them both. Slowly, he turned around, looked at Sheila, saw the tears gleaming in her eyes, and her mouth trembling as she tried not to cry.

Then, with a rough curse, he was gone.

Chapter One
Six months later

Rafe hadn't been able to find Sheila for three days. Not that he had been looking.

But when the sweet scent of plumeria started to fade from Eli's enclave, he knew something was going on.

For the past six months, he had left her alone. Realizing how close he had come to the unthinkable, he'd gone out of his way to stay away from her, giving her the distance she no doubt wanted from him. Not seeing her, not touching her, ate at him and he was slowly going out of his mind.

When he realized that she was gone, though, really gone, he just snapped. Insane fury pulsed through his veins as he tore the house apart, searching for her, growling demands at everyone in the house, only to be ignored.

Stalking into the Master's quarters with hell in his eyes probably wasn't the best way to start the day...but then again, for some odd reason, Rafe seemed to be spoiling for a fight all the time lately. It had gotten worse since that night when he had almost raped Sheila, and now it was getting impossible to control.

"Where's the little southern belle?" he demanded, flinging himself down onto a long, leather couch.

Eli glanced up from his desk just in time to see the leather molding itself to the long, rangy vampire's form.

And to see the fire in Rafe's gaze. He couldn't help the smile that filled his eyes, but he did manage to keep it from curling his lips.

"She's gone away for a while," he said, leaning back and folding his hands across his belly. "Sheila has been rather—unhappy," he decided after a moment. "She petitioned at first to leave, but we decided a vacation might suit."

"To leave?" Rafe growled.

"Yes. A new Master, she thought, a new home, might solve the problem she's been dealing with." Nothing would solve it, Eli knew, not until Rafe stopped being so bloody stubborn, but some distance might help Sheila heal a little bit.

And just might force Rafe's hand, making him do what he should have done months ago. Admit that he was in love with her.

"What problem?" Rafe demanded, shooting to his feet. "She Hunts once a week, takes Erika shopping and acts like a babysitter for the kid. And cooking. Cooking, for crying out loud. What fucking problem?"

His black hair tumbled into his eyes and he shoved it back as he started to pace, mumbling and swearing under his breath.

Eli heard every word.

"I believe she is lonely. I suggested she go find a man and get...fucked six different ways to Sunday. Well, that was Sarel's phrase. But it suits, I think," Eli said, bracing himself, and reminding himself that Rafe was a friend, and that killing him wouldn't help Rafe or Sheila's predicament.

Of course, when Rafe leaped over the desk and tore him out of his chair with startling speed, Eli did have to admit that he might have a bit more of a fight on his hands than he had previously thought. But he hadn't been planning on fighting at all. Throttling down the instinct to battle, he gave Rafe an innocent look and forced a fake bellow, "What the hell is your bloody problem?"

"You told her to what?" Rafe demanded in a low deadly whisper.

"Fuck me, she's a lovely, loving young woman. And she's *lonely*. You don't want her anymore, but nobody here will give her a damn glance for fear of insulting you. She needs a man, so I told her to go *find* one," Eli said, reaching up and shoving Rafe back.

Rafe went flying, but he took a handful of Eli's silk vest with him. Glancing down, Eli scowled. "Now that was just uncalled for. Sarel bought that for me," he snapped as he took the tattered remains off and held it up. Even Sheila with her talented hands couldn't fix this one, had she been around.

"You told her to go find a man?" Rafe repeated, his fangs protruding past his upper lip, his black eyes gleaming red in his rage.

"Aye. I did." Eli allowed a tiny smile to appear as he cocked his head. "That really shouldn't be a problem for you…but it looks like it is. Why is that?"

Rafe went completely still as he glared at Eli.

And then he stalked out.

* * * * *

Rafe couldn't believe Eli had sent Sheila off to get fucked.

You don't want her anymore... What in the hell was that bullshit? Eli knew damned good and well Sheila was the *only* thing he wanted.

She filled his days and his nights, haunted his sleep.

Not want her? Damn it, there hadn't been a day that had gone by in the last year that he hadn't wanted her.

He'd never wanted anybody the way he wanted Sheila. As he sped out of West Virginia, he promised himself he'd have her again. Soon. He'd get her to forgive him, get her to let him back into her life.

Because his was empty without her.

Bleak, cold, and empty.

* * * * *

She was in Memphis.

Rafe had been prowling around searching for her for damn near two weeks. He'd tried Georgia, tried the beaches in Miami. Knowing how the girl loved to party, he had been expecting to find her at one of her old haunts, but, no, the southern belle couldn't be that cooperative.

Shit, she wouldn't know cooperation if it bit her on the ass. His lids drooped as he recalled that fine ass, those plump rounded curves he had held as he fucked that sweet, soft body.

Not in Miami. Not in Atlanta. And she hadn't returned home to West Virginia, either. He knew, because he had bribed Mike into calling him if she so much as showed that pretty blonde head within a mile of the enclave or Eli's territory.

He had been driving through Tennessee and had an urge to head west. Driving down I-40, he planned to find a bar on Beale Street, get drunk and find some sweet thing to slake his thirst. Just feed though. Although he ached, the only woman he wanted was Sheila. And she wouldn't have him, not as things stood now anyway.

She wanted more. She wanted his heart.

But his heart had died in New York City more than a hundred and fifty years ago, the night the woman he had thought he loved had changed him into a bloody vampire. Hell, he *had* loved Sarah. Desperately. With all the passion and heart he'd had inside him.

Then she had revealed why he could only see her at night, why she wouldn't leave the life she had working as a lady of the night in the streets of New York. She had to have the sex, had to have the blood — he hadn't believed her.

It wasn't until she'd Changed him, draining him to the point of near death and then forcing her blood down his throat that he'd believed. And after she'd changed him, she'd just walked away, leaving him alone to starve and die, laughing mockingly as she'd called over her shoulder, "You are a wonderful customer, Rafe, so young, so eager and innocent. But you bore me."

That had hardened his heart until it had withered away inside his chest, rarely beating in this new life he had been forced into. He had damned near died that first day, too fucking weak to get out of the sun as dawn broke, the hunger burning through his belly, driving him nearly insane.

And then, along came Malachi. Rafe's lip curled as he recalled how pathetic he must have looked. The Scotsman had crouched by his shoulder, shaking his head, his dark blue eyes grim. "She had a bit o' fun wit' you, lad, I kin tell," he had murmured before picking Rafe up.

Rafe had snarled, "I can fucking walk on my own. Put me down, you bastard."

Mal had almost laughed. Rafe could see the amusement in his eyes, but he couldn't understand the sympathy that had stopped the mirth as the Scotsman stared at the young man whose pride and heart had been demolished. The ability to read the mind of a vampire wasn't one Rafe had ever developed, but over time, he'd realized that Malachi had that gift, among many others.

And Mal had seen. So he'd jerked him to his feet, and supported his weight, guiding him out of the alley just as the sun had started to burn down on him, scorching his flesh, sending untold agony through him.

Closing his eyes, Rafe shoved the unwelcome memories away as he hit the suburbs surrounding the outskirts of Memphis. It was two a.m., the cool October wind blew through his hair as he headed toward Beale Street.

A beer, a woman... He wanted nothing more than to relieve the ache in his cock, but he knew the touch of any woman other than the smart-assed southern belle would leave him cold.

She had no more than passed through his thoughts when he *felt* her. He shouldn't be able to feel her, sense her...a vampire, yes, he would feel that. And he did, several vampires, some Weres...but to feel one and know it was her — that shouldn't be possible.

But he did.

Running his tongue over his fangs, he drove on. As he reached Sam Cooper Boulevard the feeling grew.

Like somebody had just whispered the knowledge into his ear, Rafe knew where she was. She'd been partying all right. Just not in Miami.

Beale Street. Listening to the throb of rich blues, dancing, finding somebody to take to her bed.

He'd found her, damn it. But what in the hell was he going to do with her? He knew what he *wanted*.

Of course, what it would take to get there was anybody's guess.

* * * * *

The hot, rich taste of his blood flowed down her throat like the finest wine. Sheila felt her nipples tighten even harder as she absorbed the rush of Dom's orgasm. His hips arched as he drove his cock deep inside and held, his fingers digging into the flesh of her ass. The climax broke over her as she pulled away from his neck, leaving two small puncture wounds in his golden flesh.

Until Dom, it had been months since she had felt a man's arms around her, felt the heat of his hunger as she fucked and fed.

Dominic had been the first man, since Rafe, whose touch hadn't left her cold. There had been a few others she'd considered, but their touches had made her skin crawl.

Until Dom.

His resemblance to Rafe was unmistakable. Physically, at least.

But beyond that… Dominic was a romantic. Dominic treated her like a person, not just a fuck toy.

He was a ladies' man and he *appreciated* her, didn't want just a quick fuck from her whenever he felt horny.

Oh, she knew he wanted sex. Hell, he was a guy. But he bothered to spend time with her...had actually wanted to.

Rafe couldn't have cared less once his dick slid out of her.

With a tremendous act of will, she shoved Rafe's face from her mind as she collapsed against Dom's broad chest, the fingers of one hand absently caressing the gold hoop that ran through one nipple. He'd switched it to gold. She had shied away in instinctive fear when she'd seen it, and lied that she was allergic to silver. Well, not really a lie—silver was definitely not good for her health.

He had removed the hoop that night, and the next night there was a gold one there instead. She had greatly enjoyed tugging on that tiny piece of metal with her teeth.

"Damn—that was amazing," Dom murmured, his voice thick, sluggish. She kept the move casual as she rested her hand on his heart. She knew she hadn't taken too much, but still...the paranoia was always there.

He was a wonderful guy. He didn't deserve the life of a vampire.

She stroked her hand down his chest once she had reassured herself that he was fine. Just a little woozy.

"Mmmm...tell me. Go to sleep, baby. You had a long day," she whispered, cuddling in against him as close as she could.

"You be here when I wake up, sugar?"

She hedged. "I don't know, Dom. Depends on how late you sleep," she said, already knowing she'd be gone in a few hours. Couldn't take that chance.

But he was already asleep, the deep, steady sighs of breath escaping him as he shifted slightly on the pillow.

As she sat up, she felt it.

The anger in the air.

Anger, hell.

That was too tepid a word for what she was sensing. A deep, burning rage that battered at her mind until an artificial red seeped in—run off from his rage.

Her belly pitched and she felt the fangs that had slid back into their sheaths drive back out with a speed that startled her. *Danger...*

Rising from the bed, she tossed the heavy banner of her golden curls behind her shoulder. Damn it. Something from her world had found her here, with her lover, and it would put him in danger.

Over my dead body, she thought furiously, her eyes flying around the room, searching for the intruder she sensed, but couldn't see.

"Actually, Belle, I'd rather it be his," a low, furious voice whispered.

She spun around and saw Rafe standing at the edge of the bed, staring down at Dom with a rage so great that his eyes burned red with it. He gripped his sword in one hand, the other stroked idly up and down the edge as he stared at Dominic.

Sheila felt the fear that had flooded her dissipating as she studied Rafe. "Oh, it's just you," she said, her tone bored. Flicking her eyes to his blade, she smirked a little. "I see you still carry around your security blanket." She turned around and sauntered over to where the clothes she and Dom had discarded lay in a haphazard pile. Dom's white button-down was the closest, so she grabbed it and jammed her arms into the sleeves, turning around to see Rafe lift his gaze from the bed to stare at her.

A shiver ran down her spine at that look, but she kept her face blank. She'd given him enough emotion. She'd be damned if she gave him any more.

"Get that shirt off," he rasped, the bulge of his fangs pressing against his upper lip.

Jeez, he was pissed. She frowned at him. "What's got you so worked up? Boxers too tight?" she drawled, flopping down onto the bland couch so many hotels offered and cocking her head as she studied him.

"You are pushing your luck, Sheila. *Get the fucking shirt off. Now!*"

The rage that rolled from him came with a dominance that all but forced her to obey. But her own pride, her own anger, still so vivid after the past months, gave her the strength to ignore his demand.

"No," she replied, arching a golden brow at him and smiling. "I'm not sitting here naked in front of you, babe."

"Why not? I've seen every sweet little part of that body you just shared with him," Rafe purred. He held out the short sword and stroked the flat of it up her thigh, then touched the tip of it to one of the buttons. "Get it off."

Baring her teeth at him, she snarled, batting the sword away from her. "Would you shut up? He's pretty damned tired, but if you keep yelling, it's going to wake him up. I'd rather not have to explain why Count Dracula's cousin is looming over him," she snapped, rising from the couch and walking over to the bed to look down at Dom. Extending her mind, she touched his. She couldn't do it to many, just to those she fed on. She wasn't a powerful vampire, and suspected she wouldn't ever be.

But she made do with what she had.

He was still deep, deep asleep. With a silent command, she made sure he'd stay that way until well after dawn, when she'd have to flee. Lifting her eyes, she stared at Rafe with a patently bored look in her eyes.

"Won't you just go away?" she drawled, tossing her hair over her shoulder before planting her hands on her hips.

"Hmmm, well, I will. When I get what I came here for," he replied. His eyes were glittering and if she wasn't mistaken, his heart was kicking up, pounding with faster, harder beats.

Not as fast as a mortal's, but much faster than a vamp's heart ought to beat. He was well and truly worked up about something. She hadn't ever seen him this worked up over anything. Hell, she'd rarely seen any emotion from him...except for that last night...he had been emotional then, hot, demanding, focused... With a slight shiver, she shoved that unwelcome memory out of her mind as she drawled, "And what, pray tell, is that?"

"You."

* * * * *

Rafe saw the hot fire of fury die in her eyes, replaced by blank disbelief. It was almost comical enough to cool the rage in his gut.

Almost. Because the sweet scent of her skin that had driven him damn near insane for months had changed, mingled with the scent of another man's sweat and semen. That had him so fucking furious, he could barely breathe. Not that he really had to breathe, it was just habit. But damn it, how in the hell could she just walk away, and start fucking any man she saw?

"You are here for me... Is there some problem at home I should be aware of—wait, if that was the case, Eli can reach me very easily. Reach out and touch someone, ya know?"

Rafe flicked one last glance at the human lying unconscious on the bed, the two tiny pinprick holes in his neck already starting to shrink, thanks to the rather fantastic chemicals in a vampire's saliva. Rage ate at his gut, and he had visions of taking his blade and plunging it into the man's gut, watching as he died. He'd fucked Sheila. The bastard.

Clenching his jaw, he slid his sword back into the sheath that ran down his spine, shifting it automatically into place. If he held onto it, he didn't know if he could trust himself not to hurt that bastard, at least a little.

He walked around the bed, his eyes on her face, watching as her lashes flickered. The pulse in her neck fluttered and he caught the scent of her blood, hot and ripe, full of the power the feeding and the sex had given her. It was teasing, taunting him, that hot, sweet scent. And under it, the flat, metallic scent of male human blood. "As always, pet, you smell delicious. But I don't care for your taste in food."

Sheila gave an indelicate snort, rolling those expressive blue eyes as she spun on her heel, sauntering away. "Well, I tried to do the vegetarian diet, but it just didn't work with my metabolism," she said brightly as she lowered herself back to the couch.

Rafe's eyes flickered to the long curve of her legs as she crossed them at the knee, the shirt riding up to reveal smooth, plumply rounded thighs. Damn, but he loved her body, a woman's body, not some anorexic stick. An ass he could actually grab onto, that soft belly and her rounded hips a perfect contrast to the lean hardness of his own body. Nothing about her was hard, not her hair, not her skin, not that lush body...

Lifting his eyes, he encountered an icy blue gaze as she felt his touch and he reevaluated. Something was hard. That glint in her eyes hadn't been there before. Her eyes were cool, hard and flat as she smoothed the shirt down, covering as much of her flesh from his eyes as she could.

"Hiding from me, Belle?" he asked gently, cocking up a brow.

She slowly shook her head as she softly replied, "Hiding would imply you were trying to find me, that there was something on me you liked looking at. I wasn't enough for you to want much from me months ago. All you want is sex and you can get that anywhere. You told me that once. Nothing has changed."

Not enough? Rafe couldn't believe she had said that. *She* had thrown him out on his ass, damn it. Told him she wasn't taking his shit anymore and just turned away from him.

Well...maybe there had been something more than just her flipping out and deciding she didn't want him around. Like the fact that he didn't stay with her as they slept. How he never let himself look at her, unless he was getting her naked. How he didn't let himself touch her in public...she had gotten inside his blood. And he wouldn't let that happen again, he wouldn't let himself care for anybody. Not that the shriveled mess that was his heart would ever love again—but you could still care for somebody, and not love them.

It wasn't happening. Not to him, not again.

"Just because I'm not interested in picking out sheets or paint swatches doesn't mean I'm not interested, doll," Rafe finally said. Damn it. Why did it have to be *more*? Always more...why wasn't just the sex enough?

Sheila softly said, "I never asked for that. But it might have been nice for you to want to be with me even if our clothes weren't off."

She turned her head aside—but not fast enough. He could see the hurt in her eyes and it felt like a particularly vicious sucker punch, right to his gut. He swallowed, weighing his words carefully as he said, "It wasn't just about that."

Golden brows rose over china blue eyes. Sheila cocked her head, that pretty, rosebud mouth pursing as she studied him. "Wasn't it? You barely looked twice at me when I wasn't naked. Sorry, Rafe. But I want more than that. *Need* more than that."

"And you think this fool will give it to you?" he growled, jerking a thumb in the human's direction.

A low chuckle escaped her and she narrowed her eyes as she ran a hand through her tumbled fall of golden curls. "He's shown me more romance in a month than you showed in six."

"I'm two hundred bloody years old, Sheila," he snarled, spinning on his heel and stalking away. "I'm past the point where I play games to get horizontal with a woman."

"Hmmm. Maybe somebody should tell Sarel all the sweet things that Eli does for her are just so he can get in her pants," Sheila said drolly.

Rafe's eyes cut to her and he stopped in his tracks. "I'm not Elijah Crawford and I'm not looking to get married, pet. It's a bit different when the man and woman are married."

"So just because they are married, and we aren't, and never will be, that makes it all right for you to treat me like some kind of leper? Kiss ass, Rafe." Sheila's eyes were furious, the blue swirling from dark blue to electric blue and back again as she glared at him. He could hear her heart...smell her blood...her sex...

"I'd love to," he purred, stalking closer, grinning as she cut to the right, trying to evade him. He caught her around the waist, spinning her around and pinning her against the wall with his body, burying his face in her hair. As his cock cuddled against the soft little curve of her tummy, Rafe felt that nagging empty ache in his heart ease, just a little. Sex...just sex. And she was funny, sweet. Why shouldn't he have missed her?

Her hands wedged between them and she shoved at him, leaning away from him, her eyes snapping furiously. "Damn it, you son of a bitch, let go of me," she snapped. "You aren't doing this to me again."

Rafe felt the guilt bloom inside him and he murmured, "I'm sorry about that, pet. You know I am." Lowering his head, he nuzzled the silken cloud of her curls, holding her close against him for just a moment.

"Fine, you're sorry," she said woodenly. "Is that all?"

"No," he whispered, as that insane need from months ago rose within him once more. As he turned his head to capture her mouth, she jerked away, compressing her full mouth into a tight line. "C'mon, Belle, give me a taste," he crooned. "It's been too long..."

Almost seven months. Seven months since she had shoved him away and told him it was over. Seven months since he had tasted the wine of her blood, buried his cock in her snug heat…it seemed like seven centuries. And suddenly he had the image of him spending the rest of his life without her, the long empty years of it stretching out before him like an empty wasteland.

Alone, without her. Empty, without her.

His stomach dropped out and he felt like chaining her to his side, for all time, so she could never leave him again, so he wouldn't have to face that emptiness.

Threading his hands through her hair, he arched her neck up to his, brushing his mouth against hers.

She stood still in his arms. Oh, she was quivering, shaking like a leaf in his arms and he could smell the hot cream that had flooded her pussy.

But she didn't wrap those long, pale arms around him and she didn't open her mouth under his. Her body was still as he moved against her—*fuck*.

Lifting his head, he stared down at her, feeling his fangs as they all but throbbed in their sockets. "Is it really over, Belle?"

Lowering her lashes, she pushed at his shoulders insistently, until he had to either let her go, or risk hurting her. "This isn't what I want, Rafe."

His nostrils flared, the scent of her flooding his head. "You want me to believe you don't want me?" he demanded, his voice low and angry.

"It has nothing to do with whether or not my body wants sex with you," she whispered. "It has to do with what *I* want. And I don't want to be treated like a toy anymore, something you can take out and play with when the mood suits you. And somebody you can ignore whenever you feel like it."

She walked away, lowering herself onto the bed and Rafe could have howled at the fury that ripped through him, seeing her so close to the human. She had fucked him... Rafe had watched with equal parts of fury and desire as she rose from his neck, the orgasm tearing through her as she screamed. Not ripping her away from the mortal had taken every bit of will he had in his body, and his control was shot.

And still, she sat there, her body covered in a shirt that her human lover had worn, her eyes cool and blank as she stared at him, refusing to give in to the call of her body.

He prowled around the room, hands clenching into tight fists. *Damn it. Damn it.*

Damn it. There was rage inside him, restlessness, a hunger that was all but driving him insane and the one being on earth who could quiet him didn't want him touching her.

He stopped in mid-pace and spun around, staring at her.

No. She wanted him.

She just didn't want to.

She saw something on his face just a second before he moved, but she didn't react fast enough. As he pulled her off the bed, jerking her up against him, Rafe felt the response tear through her, felt the imperceptible softening of her body and he knew she'd hate how easily he could read her.

Catching her head in his hands, he stared down at her, eyes hooded, face stark. "I've gone insane since you left me. I need you—know that," he rasped, then he slanted his mouth across hers, wrapping his arms around her and lifting her, carrying her away from the bed, over to the balcony where he kicked the door open.

Away from the scents of sex, blood and Dominic. Away from the man she had allowed inside her body. Damn it, he could *smell* the human. It drove him insane, teased the raging animal of anger inside him—and underneath it all was her scent. That scent he hadn't been able to get out of his head.

As he moved his mouth down her neck, he heard her gasp. Her nails bit into his shoulders and he growled low in his throat as her hips moved unconsciously against his.

He couldn't believe he had lived without this, not for even a day. He wasn't doing it again.

* * * * *

Sheila felt the decision, more than saw it. She saw his eyes go from fury to determination, but she didn't jerk away from him quickly enough. His hands, hard and determined, pulled her against him, off the bed, into his arms. Those steely hard lengths wrapped around her, as he lifted her, covering her mouth, swallowing her furious demands that he let her go.

She shoved hard at his shoulders as he moved the brand of his mouth down her neck, scalding her with his touch. "Damn it, Rafe, don't you *listen*?" she snapped.

And then he sank his teeth into her neck as he pinned her against the brick wall of the balcony. A whimper left her as he started to pump his cock against her belly, one big hand cupping her hip and holding her steady as his teeth pierced her flesh.

"Rafe…" she whimpered. *Rafe…*

For the first time in months, something inside her felt whole. But her heart was breaking, even as her body yielded to his. He'd never change, but just a quick fuck every now and then wasn't enough.

Well, knowing Rafe, it would be more than one fuck, and only the first one would be quick... Once he eased that driving hunger, he liked to take his time...

The low, strangled sound came to their ears. Sheila stilled as it sounded again just as Rafe was reaching for the collar of her shirt.

His hand clenched into a tight fist as he swore furiously in Italian, cocking his head and listening.

The heat of his gaze left a sizzling path along her skin as he raised his eyes from her neck, along her jaw to her eyes. "Get inside, Belle. We'll finish this later."

She snorted as he turned and leaped off the balcony, the long tails of his coat flapping around him as he hurtled to the ground four stories down. "As if," she murmured, stalking into the hotel room and snagging her jeans. She wasn't a bloody Master, but she *was* a Hunter.

And that sob had sounded so tortured...almost drowning out the rough, male laughter.

She had to drop a few levels before she jumped. Her bones were dense but Sheila had only been a Vampire for twenty years. She wasn't as tough as the older ones, might never be.

But she was still a damned Hunter and he could expect her to hide away all he wanted. But that didn't mean she'd do it. Following the almost inaudible sounds of struggle, her own fury started to rise.

She was a Hunter. A good one.

So what if she didn't look the part quite as much as Rafe, who had grabbed one man and flung him against the wall, before spinning around, that long black coat flying around him like a cape as he pounced on the second man who was still trying to figure out where his buddy had gone.

One second, they'd been tearing the clothes off the girl lying there, two holding her arms, the other fumbling at his fly.

The first one was probably dead, Sheila knew. His head had hit the brick wall with a sickening thud. She smelled blood, but there was very little on the ground—just the bare whisper of a heartbeat. The medical examiners would most like find a cerebral hemorrhage, she guessed.

Rafe had the second one pinned against the wall, drawing his head back to strike. As the third one wised up, deciding to take off, he turned and barreled straight into Sheila. "Where ya going, honey?" she asked sweetly as he tried to knock her aside.

"Get out of my way, bitch!" he shrieked.

Sheila laughed and reached out, grabbing the collar of the thick leather jacket and jerking him against her. Flashing him a toothy smile, she whispered, "Say goodnight, honey."

Now, Dominic's blood had filled her belly like warm honey.

But this...this was a drug, intoxicating, rich, mind-blowing. She wanted to kill. Badly. As he struggled, she wrapped one arm around him, crushing him against her, unaware of the odd change in the air around her as she fed. Unaware of almost everything—this was sweet, possibly the sweetest she'd ever had.

Except...her victim was getting a hard-on. She felt it against her belly as his struggles ceased and he started to reach for her. A greedy moan fell from him as he clutched at her hips.

The feel of his dick against her belly forced its way through the hunger-induced fog that had flooded her brain. "Eeeewwww!" She shoved him away and watched as he went flying to the ground several feet away, his eyes hot and heavy on her face.

"What in the fuck?" she demanded, scrubbing her hand over the back of her mouth, that sweet taste of his blood suddenly foul on her tongue. "I don't want some would-be rapist pawing me."

A soft chuckle echoed in her ear and she turned around, glaring up at Rafe. "What is so damned funny, slick?" she demanded.

"Well...you're enough to give a dead man a hard-on, pet. But all that aside..." His hand lifted, hovering just above her face, his lids drooping low as raw hunger etched his face. "You're getting more powerful...just took a grand leap there."

"What?" Then she shook her head, and in a louder, more emphatic voice, she said, "No. I don't want more power. I like how I am, thank you."

"Then you need to stop Hunting. The more you Hunt, the more powerful you will get," Rafe drawled. Then his eyes cut to her face, glinting with fury. "Didn't I tell you to stay?"

"Actually, no. You said we'd finish it later. But since I'm not welcome, *you* clean up." She went to the woman's side, finding her asleep.

Rafe, most likely. There was the lingering feel of vamp magick in the air, something she didn't possess yet—didn't really want to possess. More power was more responsibility. Taking the woman in her arms, she turned and stalked away.

Chapter Two

Sheila had been flopping in a friend's house for a couple of weeks. Kelsey was in Europe for a while—the offer of the house had been a Godsend. The witch was a quiet, reserved lady with eyes that seemed to see clear through you. She had seen through Sheila quickly enough, when she stopped briefly by Excelsior before making her trip to the old grounds.

Trouble's coming, she had said obliquely, shrugging before flipping her habitual red braids over her shoulders as she ignored Malachi's hailing.

Sheila had fought not to snicker at the affronted look on the ancient one's face. Now, Leandra hadn't made the effort to smother her laughter. She had just laughed, very amused by Malachi's obvious disgruntlement. "Dat man dere, he don't know what he be wantin'," she drawled, shaking her head as her dark eyes danced with mirth. "Women throw themselves at his feet and he ignores it—but dat woman won't throw herself at his feet, and he can't figure out why."

Kelsey rolled her pretty brown eyes, the gold in those eyes seeming to glint as she replied cuttingly, "Because it requires more than a sexy vampire to make me forget myself?" With that, Kelsey had dismissed Leandra and Malachi, as though they weren't even in the room.

Then she offered her house in Memphis to Sheila. "I don't live there. It was…a friend's, so I can't sell it, but I don't go there. Haven't been to Memphis in shoot, thirty years, I think," she mused, her eyes distant. "But it's clean, well-kept. I have a lady who goes in once a week to clean. I usually rent it out, but lately that's too much trouble."

So Sheila had landed there. And the best part...Kelsey had smiled at her with a mischievous glint in her eyes that at the time hadn't made sense. "Rafe's never been there, baby," the witch had told her.

So even if he did, by some slim chance find her again, he was stuck. Because unless Kelsey came by from Europe to invite him in, he was locked out. Well, Sheila had been living there long enough that some of her own essence had seeped into the simple hearth magick that locked the unwelcome from a person's home.

It was entirely possible that *she* could invite him in, at that point.

Except she was more likely to sprout wings and fly.

She moved slowly into the basement, her fingers trailing down the carved wooden banister, her eyes roaming over the familiar house. Even though it had been redecorated, and recently, she still smelled smoke in the air. Something awful had happened here once. She didn't know what, didn't know if Kelsey would ever tell her.

But she suspected the *friend* the house belonged to had been more than a friend. A lover, maybe. Family, possibly. And they'd died here in this house, in a fire.

There was nothing evil in the house, nothing left over. But Sheila suspected that hadn't always been the case. Houses this old tended to harbor something from their previous occupants, anger, love, sadness... Houses had memories, just like people did.

But this one was wiped clean, like a slate. Too clean. Kelsey had done something here, maybe guided somebody into the afterlife. Maybe something more, maybe something less.

All in all, though, the faint scent of smoke aside, this was the most peaceful haven she'd stayed at in quite some time.

With a sigh, she cuddled into the bed that was tucked under the staircase, thick black drapes hanging from the posts kept her shrouded in darkness. Kelsey had offered to come in and sun-proof the house for her, but Sheila couldn't stand the thought of sleeping someplace without windows, where sunlight never penetrated.

This worked just fine. Sheltered from the windows in the basement by the corner at the end of the short walkway, her bed was nestled in the alcove under the steps. Even on the sunniest days, little sunlight penetrated the hallway. The drapes were just an added protection, more for her peace of mind than necessity. Unless she got out of bed and walked to the end of the hall during daylight, and stood in the rays pouring through, the sun was no threat to her.

Now if she was unlucky enough to get caught in the sunlight, it would kill her. She had only been dead two decades, and until she reached her first century, direct sunlight was fatal.

Sheila had a hard time staying awake during the day anyway. Right now, before the sun even started to lighten the eastern sky, her eyes were heavy and fatigue flooded her mind.

Cuddling against her pillow, Sheila closed her eyes and slept.

He haunted her, even in her dreams. In her dreams, the laws of magick that kept him from entering the house were no barrier to him and he came down the stairs as she slept, moving up on the bed, drawing back the bed curtains to stare at her.

In her dream, a soft moan escaped her as his body came down beside her, one long-fingered hand stroking down the length of her nude body. His mouth covered hers and she whimpered in pleasure as he plunged his tongue inside her body and one hand cupped the round curves of one breast. His fingers milked the nipple as he moved to hover over her, pushing his thigh between hers, spreading her legs wide before he fit his cock into the notch between her thighs, pumping his denim-covered hips back and forth in a slow, tormenting rhythm that teased her clit, inflamed her senses, and stole her breath.

Caught in the dream, she rolled to her side, plunging one hand between her thighs, stroking her fingers over the hard bud of her clit, while in her dream, Rafe freed his cock, driving into her with one hard thrust. She climaxed with a broken cry…then rolled onto her belly, slipping into a dark, dreamless sleep.

* * * * *

Rafe came to a sudden halt, hissing out a breath between his teeth as images slammed into his mind. A bed made of dark wood, tucked under a narrow staircase, surrounded by thick black swaths of velvet. Brushing it aside, finding his southern belle there, sleeping, her sweet, lushly curved body displayed on the black velvet of the comforter, glowing ivory against all that blackness. Covering her body with his, kissing her…fucking her until she came around him with a cry.

His fangs dropped as he slowed to a halt outside the hotel where he had found Sheila. Lust ate a hole in his belly, the need to feel that soft smooth body with its plump curves pressed against his, driving him nearly insane.

Sliding his tongue over his lips, he drew in the air around him, searching for that faint, teasing scent. Lust blistered into rage as he found nothing.

She wasn't there.

She had taken off running—and it had never occurred to him that she wouldn't go there. Never occurred to him to find out where she stayed during the day. And she wasn't there.

His rage exploded into a supernova as somebody shambled out of the hotel, a sated, goofy smile on his young face.

The human she had been fucking...Dominic, she had called him. Right as he drove his cock into her pussy, gripping her soft white thighs in his hands.

Eyes gleaming, he shifted to mist and followed the mortal.

* * * * *

Sheila left Kelsey's house early that evening, breathing in the rich scent of fall, the river, the night.

The air was cool and fresh against her skin as she tucked her hands into her pockets, her feet slapping lightly against the pavement.

The idle thought moved through her brain that by leaving the house, she was just asking to run into Rafe again. She really didn't want that. Every time she looked at him it made her heart bleed. She had no idea what had brought the brooding bastard here, but she was ready for him to leave.

However, that sure as hell didn't mean she was going to linger in her house until he got the hell out of Memphis. She loved this town, and she was going to enjoy it for as long as she could. Especially Beale Street. As she turned the corner and the lights of Beale Street exploded in front of her, she grinned, walking a little faster.

But a few blocks shy of it, her steps faltered as the scent of something familiar filled her head.

Dominic…

She smelled blood. A lot of it. And it was Dominic's. Her heart froze inside her chest as she started to jog along the sidewalk, following the scent. When she got there, there was a cold fist of fear lodged in her throat. The scent of blood was too strong on the air. Too much blood. How did a human survive that much blood loss?

The stink of it was so strong that, for a long moment, she didn't smell what else was there. When it hit her, she slammed a hand against the wall, her mind whirling. *Vampire.*

Rafe.

He had been there. Close, very close to Dominic. Her eyes lifted to the barricaded ally just across the street, the red and blue lights from the police car flashing across her face. He wouldn't.

But damn it, she smelled him. He *couldn't*. She licked her lips, taking a few steps closer, forcing a bland, curious expression on her face as she mingled with the people standing across the street, whispering amongst themselves.

"What's going on over there?" she asked, hoping her voice wasn't shaking as much as she suspected it was.

Nobody glanced twice at her as one guy murmured, "Somebody got creamed, lady. Totally. But the body isn't there. But the blood…man, you can smell it from here."

Rubbing her temple, she fought to control the sick feeling in her gut. "Who was it, does anybody know?"

Somebody answered, flicking her glance. "Nobody knows. Like the man said, there's no body. Lady in the store there heard some commotion and she called the cops. But nobody saw anything. When the cops got here all they found was that alley, torn up, blood all over the place."

No body.

No body. She mumbled something under her breath and pulled back, slowly retreating and working her way around to the back of one of the closed shops on her side of the street. She glanced around, listening to make sure nobody was nearby.

Then she crouched down, tensed her muscles and leaped upward, catching the bottom of the fire escape on the second floor. Her fingers closed on the rough metal of the grate and she grimaced as it bit into her hands. As she hauled herself up, she muttered, "There's got to be some place around here where I can get a manicure."

The humor was a weak attempt to force the worry from her mind as she ran lightly along the roof of the building. She took a breath and leaped across the ten feet that separated the buildings, grimacing as she lost her balance and nearly crashed face-first into the gravel as she landed.

Slowing to a halt, she moved to the shadows, glancing around. The cops hadn't come up here yet, but they would, soon. Although she hadn't mastered the vampire magicks that let her change her shape, she knew the shadows. Knew how to use them, could even make them seem to thicken around her when she needed to hide. Sliding to the back of the building, she stared down, listening.

After a minute, she turned away, hands propped on her hips. They didn't have a damned clue. She could smell Rafe, smell Dominic.

There was a scent she didn't recognize, but the more familiar ones of the two men crowded her brain, her senses until she could think of nothing else.

She backtracked, following the faint scent in the air. The scent was Rafe's. There was no blood trail, no overpowering scent of blood to follow and it made no sense. That much blood should flood the air. Why couldn't she scent it?

So she followed Rafe, the hot, musky taste of the man who always had the ability to make the spit in her mouth dry up.

When the street opened up below her and she had no more buildings to leap across, she moved back to the rear part of the building, and jogged down the fire escape on silent feet.

Rafe...you wouldn't have. There was no reason. Hunters didn't kill. And Dominic was the sweetest damn soul, harmless.

But a part of her remembered the red gleam of anger in Rafe's black eyes.

* * * * *

Rafe lifted his lashes, stroking one hand down the soft smooth neck of a lady by the name of Cora. She was sweet, young, and now sleeping soundly in his arms as he eased her back down to the hood of the car. The wind came blowing off the river, but it couldn't carry away the soft, sweet scent of woman.

Sheila. Slowly, he turned around and saw her standing there, her eyes bright, glowing a deep, electric blue, the wind blowing thick streamers of hair across her face, along her neck, the ends of the golden strands curling around the tips of her breasts.

"Hello, sweet Southern Belle," he purred, licking away a drop of blood from the corner of his mouth. "I would have invited you out for a bite, but I couldn't track you down."

Sheila's eyes, dark and unreadable, dropped to Cora's smiling face, listening to the soft little snores that escaped her. Rafe had to bite back a scowl as Sheila studied Cora's body, sprawled boneless, and still fully clothed, on the hood of his car. One golden brow lifted and she asked softly, "This your first bite of the night?"

Rafe shrugged. "I don't need much, Belle. And she was a sweet little thing," he added, flashing a toothy smile at her.

"What about Dominic?" she asked woodenly.

Rafe scowled at her. "Damn it, Belle, you would have to go mention that bastard. What did you do, go get yourself a fuck before you came here to taunt me?"

She cocked her head as she stared at him. "You haven't seen him? Not since you left the hotel room?" she asked, straightening her head and sauntering forward, that thick golden hair sliding around her shoulder and gleaming under the moonlight. "Not once?"

Rafe's brows drew low over his eyes. "Well, hell. I saw him this morning. He was leaving the hotel you two were so cozy at," he snapped, stalking up to her, cupping her softly rounded chin in his palm. "Had a smile on his face that I know very well. You've left me with that smile, once or twice."

Sheila's lashes lowered over her eyes and she said softly, "Rafe, that's bullshit. You never smile. Especially not over me."

His heart wrenched at the pain that moved through her eyes. Quietly, he told her, "Now that's where you're wrong. You made me smile more than anybody else ever has in my life. Then you told me to stay the hell away from you, and I couldn't remember how to smile again." He threaded his fingers through her hair, arched her heart-shaped face up to his gaze, and rubbed one thumb over her lips. "When Eli told me you had left, something died inside me."

A tiny smile curved her lips. He watched as she reached up and patted his cheek. "Poor Rafe." Those pretty eyes turned cold and cynical and she jerked away, walking with that same, slow sway of hip that had driven him mad for months. "I think Dominic is dead."

For a long moment, her words didn't register as he tried to make sense of how unlike herself she was acting. Sheila was soft, sweet and warm, with no desire to become a more powerful Hunter, no desire to be anything more than what she was.

But this woman in front of him was hard, cold and angry. Feelings he had ever associated with her.

Finally, those words connected to the others and made sense in his head. *I think Dominic is dead.* Narrowing his eyes on the long line of her back, he asked, "Why do you think that?"

She laughed, a sound that had a wild ring to it. "Probably because there's too much of his blood splattered in an alley back by the Peabody. The air reeks with it—with blood, anger…violence. So much blood. A human can't live after losing that much blood. But there's no body," she said hollowly.

Understanding hit him like a load of bricks and he closed the distance between them in three long strides, closing one hand around her shoulder and spinning her around. "You think I could have done that?" he demanded, bending down until his face was level with hers.

One brow rose and she shrugged, lifting one shoulder carelessly, her eyes unreadable. "Your scent was all over the place. I recognized two of the scents there—yours…and Dominic's blood."

That was when he realized two things.

She thought he could have murdered an innocent man.

And he was shit-faced in love with her, and had been from the beginning.

The knowledge hit like a fist in the gut. The bottom of his stomach dropped out, falling to his feet and leaving his heart feeling hollow and empty.

Sourly, he muttered, "I sure as hell have left you with a nice opinion of me, haven't I, Sheila?"

Softly, she said, "You didn't see the look on your face when I saw you standing over us. I did. If we could have heart attacks, I'd most likely be dead now."

He reached out, cupping the back of her neck and hauling her against him. "I would *never* hurt you," he rasped, enraged.

Tears welled in her eyes as she replied in a thick voice, "Rafe, you already have. Are you so blind you can't see that?" Then she forced a bitter smile as she added, "But it's not me I'm worried about."

There was a soft little moan from behind him and he slowly released Sheila, staring at her with dark, shuttered eyes. *You already have...* He swallowed, the bitter taste of regret heavy in his mouth.

Slowly, he turned back to Cora, focusing on the rise and fall of her chest, the soft sound of her breathing. Once he had swallowed down the anger, he said, "We need to find your friend, Dominic, Belle. If it was bad enough that you think a vampire could have done it, he may be in trouble."

Sheila whispered, "Too much blood. A human can't survive that." He heard the trembling in her voice, the ache of remembered pain, and he wanted nothing more than to wrap his arms around her and soothe it away, kiss that soft mouth until she leaned into him, hungry, her mind empty of everything but him.

He didn't have the right, though. Shoving a hand through his hair, he forced the tormenting thoughts out of his head as he said, "Whatever happened to him, we've got an obligation to find out. Somebody who can be that brutal needs to die."

Slowly, he turned and stared at her. "Or do you still think I did it?"

Chapter Three

No. Sheila scowled as she got into the backseat of Rafe's classic '57 Bel Air, slid across the bench seat until she could recline, and crossed her feet at the ankle, taking perverse pleasure when the heels of her boots scuffed against the door.

No, she didn't think he'd killed Dominic. In her heart, she hadn't really ever thought it. It was the mind that tripped her up—in her mind, she couldn't help the little suspicion. And why in the hell should she care if she saw the gleam of hurt in his dark eyes before he shuttered them against her?

I shouldn't, she insisted, her lower lip poking out as she crossed her arms over her chest and stared out the window. *How many times has he pushed me away? Too many to count.* When she had told him to stay away, he hadn't even cared enough to try to change her mind.

And she had been gone for more than three long months before he decided to come looking for her. *Three months.* Hell, she knew she'd been going out of her way to avoid him. They'd go weeks without even seeing the other's face, but three months for him to come looking for her?

She'd spent nearly a month at Excelsior before coming to Memphis. And he hadn't ever shown up there to look for her. And it wasn't like she was hard to find. A couple of questions and he would have found her. She hadn't told anybody there not to tell him. He'd just never bothered to ask.

Because he didn't care.

A shiver raced down her spine as she remembered the infuriated, possessive look in his dark eyes as he had stood over her and Dominic. Was that the look a man had when he didn't care?

She didn't know.

But she did know she was tired of Rafe's pendulous moods, swinging from wanting her to pushing her away, to insane fury when another man looked at her. Either he wanted her or he didn't.

A thoughtful frown crossed her face as she recalled the woman he had laid on the hood of his car, her face relaxed in sleep, a tiny smile on her mouth, her body fully dressed.

From what she could tell, he hadn't even tried to get her clothes off.

Rafe feeding from a woman without fucking her. That was unlike him, very unlike him. Before they had gotten together, there was rarely a night when Rafe hadn't returned from his patrol in town, smelling of female blood and sex.

A flare of remembered jealousy raced through her. He had stopped taking every woman he saw to bed with him while they were together, but that had to have changed by now. Abstinence wasn't something he was familiar with.

Her lips curled in a slow, bitter smile as she recalled the stunned anger that had been in his eyes as he'd stood over her and Dominic. Chances were, he had expected her to be mourning him too much to go looking for a man to warm her bed. *Yeah. Right.*

Granted, it had taken a little while before she had been interested. Dominic had been the only one who had interested more than her eye. His sly wit and that romantic streak of his had tugged at her heartstrings.

Tears stung her eyes as she recalled the devastation in the alley. Where was he?

The car slowed to a stop and she heard Rafe swear softly as he banged his head, getting his date out of the car. Nothing like a limp body.

Something hot and sour twisted in her belly...*a limp body*. Before she could block the picture out, the image of Dominic, his body lifeless and still, flashed before her eyes and she had to clap a hand over her mouth to keep from whimpering aloud.

"You really care about him."

At the sound of Rafe's cold, flat voice, she looked up, unaware that tears were gleaming in her eyes. "Yes." A slight scowl crossed her face and she shrugged. "Unlike some people, I don't feel the need to fuck every time I feed. I prefer to have some sort of connection," she said waspishly.

In the mirror, she could see just the upper part of Rafe's face as he watched her. One black brow lifted and he shrugged one broad shoulder. "I don't believe you came across me fucking anybody today, did you?"

She blinked. "What, are you turning over a new leaf?" she muttered. Turning her head, she stared out the back window, feeling oddly cold.

"I haven't wanted another woman since you, Belle," he whispered, his voice hot, sweet, reaching out and stroking her skin like a hand.

Flashing him a narrow glance, she snickered, "Yeah, right."

He just stared at her, his eyes intense. After a moment, she swallowed, her throat tight and dry. "You expect me to believe you haven't been with anybody since we split, Rafe? I'm not stupid, darlin'," she drawled, even as a hot, indescribable emotion settled in her belly.

"Never said you were. A little blind at times, but I never thought you were stupid."

Sheila tore her gaze away from his, forcing herself to stare back outside. His words echoed inside her mind — even though she tried to tell herself it was bullshit.

"Know anybody who would want to hurt your Dominic?" Rafe asked levelly, with just the slightest sneer on his face.

Sheila rested her head against the window behind her, sighing tiredly. "He's a sweet guy — not a mean bone in his body. If he has any enemies at all, it would surprise the hell out of me." Rafe had the window down and her hair, colorless in the moonlight, whipped into her eyes. She caught the thick locks in her hand, holding it in a loose tail with her fist.

"Maybe it wasn't him they were out to get."

Her eyes flew to meet his in the mirror and she scowled, her golden brows drawing low over her eyes as she demanded, "What in the world does *that* mean?"

He shrugged negligently. "If he's as good as all that, then there's no reason to want him dead. And you said there was violence in the air. Violence is heat. Anger and rage breed heat. If it was as bad as you're making me think, then it only makes sense that somebody with a lot of rage inside them hurt your sweetheart."

Sheila had to bite back the words, *he's not my sweetheart*. She hadn't planned on spending more than a few days with Dominic.

Still…wasn't it better if Rafe thought she was taken? Hooked up with somebody else? Then he wouldn't be trying to seduce his way back into her bed — well, maybe.

Closing her eyes, she whispered, "That doesn't make any sense."

Rafe said quietly, "It does if it's somebody who knows he's gotten very close to a Hunter."

Her eyes flew open, spine stiffening as she spun around in the seat, staring straight ahead. "No." She swallowed convulsively, her eyes tearing, burning. "*No.*"

* * * * *

Rafe hated himself the second he said it, although he suspected in his gut that was exactly what had happened. He had followed that bastard Dominic, rage eating his gut into pieces. The longer he had watched Dominic, the more he had hated him, and the more foolish he had felt.

He'd bought Sheila a stuffed animal.

Rafe had stood staring into the shop, watching as Dominic went in and pointed out the silly panda bear in the window, the one holding a rose in its chubby paw, and bought it for her.

Sheila loved pandas. Rafe hadn't ever bought her a damned thing. Six months together and he'd never bought her anything. Then that grinning human had walked into her life, made her smile, bought her pandas.

He had talked about her to the salesclerk. Rafe could hear them, the girl obviously flirting with the good looking kid, but he was oblivious, replying that *No, not for a girl. A lady…sweetest lady you'll ever meet…*

Yes. That was Sheila.

And now she was sitting in the backseat of his Chevy with hot tears pouring down her face and her heart kicking up to a rapid pace of fifty beats a minute.

"Sheila."

Her lashes lowered for a long moment and then she opened her eyes to stare at him, that pretty mouth set in an unhappy, fearful line.

"If anything has happened to him, we'll find the people responsible," he said softly. It wouldn't change what had happened.

But in his gut, he felt he owed her that, at least. Whoever it was would pay for putting that pain in her eyes, for taking away somebody who had put a smile on her face.

* * * * *

He was alive—barely, Ella thought, sighing tiredly as she brushed her stringy, tangled hair away from her face. It had been touch and go for a while. His body had fought the change at first, but with help from Robbie, they had guided him across.

The flat taste of his blood in her mouth reminded her of just how weak he was. Such low blood volume left the blood flat on the palate. She'd fed him, hating every second of it.

But he was alive.

That was what counted.

The bastard had lost this one.

Rising from the bed, she headed out of the room, glancing up as Robbie jerked up from where he had fallen asleep on the floor. His dirty face told her he had forgotten to take a bath again. The dirt was from the spells he had cast to help guide the newly changed vampire over, and from more shields of protection.

Protection—would they work? Rubbing vigorously at her arms, she prayed so. Robbie was a damned powerful witch—but he was…slow. Not that he could help it. How a witch of his power had been born into the body of a half-wit, she didn't know.

Between his power though, and her brain, they weren't a bad pair.

"Robbie, honey, you need to go wash your face. Take a bath, eat something," she reminded him with a forced smile.

As he rose, he smiled down at her, that bright guileless smile only children and the very innocent have, a smile that said "all is well in the world". Never mind that they had a monster breathing down their necks, and now a new burden in the form of a newly changed vampire.

She wasn't really worried about the vampire. His heart was pure. She'd felt it when she'd fed him, and prayed her blood would be strong enough.

Weak. Useless.

Ella shoved the hateful voice away and sighed, turning away from Robbie as he walked silently into the bathroom. As the water splashed on, Ella stared at her reflection. It wasn't true that vampires had no reflection, although she wished desperately the legend was true.

If it was, she wouldn't have to see her reflection, that stunted form, forever caught in the body of a teenaged girl just edging on the cusp of womanhood. Wouldn't have to see the hideous scarring of her face, the vicious scar that ran from her eye, downward to her mouth, causing the right side of it to pucker down in a perpetual frown, wouldn't have to see the empty socket on the left where once a lovely eye of iris purple had been.

A bear had mauled her, more than four hundred years ago, when she had been out in the forests near her parents' house, just ten years old. Mauled her, blinded her on one side.

At the time, she had thought that had been the worst thing that had ever happened to her.

But when she was fifteen, something even worse happened. Ella had heard her mother's dreamy, entranced voice answering somebody who had called out to her. Tumbling out of bed, she'd run to her mama's side, begging her not to listen to that voice. It was evil, no matter how sweet it had sounded.

But Mary White had invited the man in, as he had requested. Ella had grabbed the poker from the fireplace, jabbing it at the green-eyed man with flowing blond hair, his heavy French accent thickening his words and sending cold chills down her spine as he spoke. One blow from his hand had knocked her aside and she'd passed out.

When she woke up, her mother was dead, and the bastard was leaning over *her*, whispering in Ella's ear, murmuring about what a fun pet she would be.

It had taken two hundred years to break free from him. Two hundred years and help from the witch Pierre had brought into his house. Robbie was the half-breed child of an Indian brave and a white woman. They'd fallen in love, best as Ella could tell from the information she had gathered over the years, but her family had learned of it, and when the Indian had come to get his bride, he'd found her beaten and nearly dead. In his anger to avenge her, he'd run headlong into the business end of the father and brother's rifles.

They'd killed him—but paid for that mistake when the man's tribe had swarmed upon them in the dead of night, killing the men, and leaving the mother alone as they took Robbie's mama back with them.

That he'd lived was nothing short of a miracle. But he was born damaged. His mind was forever that of a child.

How long ago that had been, Ella couldn't say, because Robbie, like many powerful witches, seemed ageless. He had looked to be in his twenties when they'd first met, and he hadn't seemed to age at all.

In any way. His mind was still that of a youth and his ways terribly simple. When coaxed into using his magick, he would use it, but since Pierre, it took more and more to convince him to use it. Pierre had abused the witch's magick terribly. Robbie was afraid it of now.

Weary, Ella lay down on her bed, secure in the darkness. The sun rose higher and higher on the horizon and exhaustion pulled at her. But it took a great deal before she was able to rest.

She couldn't understand why Pierre had gone after this mortal. Couldn't understand it at all.

But it had been Pierre.

She'd know his scent anywhere.

* * * * *

In her fury, Sheila's fangs slid from their sockets, bulging just slightly under her upper lip. The cops had finally left the crime scene, so they could now venture into it and try to find something that would help them.

But nothing was there.

Nothing but the yellow security tape, the liberal splashes of dried blood on the street, and the brick wall of the building where Sheila had crouched hours earlier. No footsteps, no trail, no sign of anything.

"What kind of vampire could move without leaving a trail?" Rafe whispered. "We should be able to smell him. But all I smell is…" He lifted his head, drawing in deep draughts of air, his lids low over his eyes. "Human, pain…magick." His eyes moved to Sheila's and he cocked a brow. "Did you smell the magick?"

She scowled at him, lifting a shoulder. "I smelled something I didn't recognize. I haven't been around magick as much as you have. So why is there magick in the air?"

Rafe flashed a toothy grin. "Easy. There was no way to move anybody who was bleeding as much as Dominic was without leaving some scent, or a blood trail. *Something.* Unless they used magick."

She caught the tip of her tongue between her teeth, cocking her head as she studied the alley. "So there was somebody here with the vampire? Helping him?"

Rafe frowned, shaking his head. "No, I don't think so. That would be dark magick. Dark magick leaves a mark on the air. I don't feel anything like the stink dark magick leaves behind. Maybe somebody came behind and found him, took him someplace to take care of him."

"Why hide themselves?" Sheila demanded. "If they did that, they hid their trail, otherwise we'd be able to track Dominic."

Rafe rolled his eyes at her. "Pet, whoever hurt him wasn't exactly a nice person. Maybe this witch didn't want to be found."

Sheila rubbed her hands over her arms, guilt and grief gnawing a hole in her belly. She had to press her lips together to keep them from trembling as she studied the nasty bloom of rust red all over the place.

"Whose territory is this? Anybody's?"

"Not that I know of. There's a Hunter close to Nashville, a werewolf and his pack. A small enclave in the Smokies. And a witch in Little Rock. Far as I know, though, nobody has claimed this piece of land," he said. Grimly, he added, "We'd better hope not—otherwise we have a killer loose here and a Hunter who isn't taking care of it."

She lifted a curious brow at him.

Rafe murmured, "Whenever some awful crime against nature happens, the earth feels it. And the land is connected to the master. If there was one here, he or she would have already shown up. Besides, I'd have raised a blip on the radar when I came into town. Eli says he can feel any new vampire that comes into his territory and the older the vampire, the more powerful the urging he has to check the person out. Same for shifters and witches. You feel it when somebody is in your territory. Goes hand in hand with being able to protect it."

Sheila studied him. "How come you're so sure it was a paranormal that did it? Humans are capable of pretty nasty evils."

Her eyes dropped unwittingly to his mouth as it curled in a sexy snarl. Damn...she loved that mouth. She had to force herself to focus on what he was saying, and away from the shape of his lips, the memory of them on her body.

"Just a funny feeling." He shook his head. "I can't explain it. But I can feel when there's been a vampire, or a shifter, around. I can't track him, but I know when I'm in the area of others like us. Comes with time. This wasn't a human attack. And Dominic looks pretty strong. The average person wouldn't be able to take him by surprise to do this kind of damage, without Dominic hurting him back. If that had happened, we'd smell somebody else's blood."

In the distance, they heard a car and the skin on Sheila's nape pricked. "I think we need to go. The cops are bound to come back here and I'd rather them not find us here," she said, tucking her hands in her pockets and withdrawing further into the shadows as Rafe cast one last look around.

Then they left the same way they had come, taking the fire escapes silently and retreating along the building roofs. She glanced down before she followed Rafe and saw a nondescript Crown Vic stop at the mouth of the alley. A man with world-weary eyes climbed from it.

Cops, she thought with a curl of her lip. Leaving just in time.

Chapter Four

The streets were oddly quiet.

Rafe decided he really didn't like the silence. Although he generally preferred to be left alone, and liked silence, this didn't feel natural.

This was a large city. Lots of youth here. Lots of life. Places like this drew those who lived through others. Hell, New Orleans had a vampire population that was second to none in the country. He'd expected Memphis to be the same way.

But he'd sensed only a few vampires. Should be more than that. Not necessarily an Enclave of Hunters—the land tended to chose its own Master and wouldn't welcome just any vampire. But certainly, he'd expected to feel more than just a few vamps here and there.

But he hadn't expected to feel one who was so evil, so powerful that it made him want to leave. Whoever had done this had been a Master. And an evil one, to boot. The internal urge to get away from somebody stronger than him was instinctive—he should be wanting to flee.

But he couldn't even sense the bastard.

That really worried him.

Sheila moved along the streets a few blocks over, watching, as he walked down Main Street. He could feel her, feel the pulse beating in her throat, feel the buzz of sated hunger that coursed through her veins.

She'd fed.

As young as she was, she needed to feed more often, so she had gone sauntering into a club on Beale Street, while he watched from the shadows, jealousy eating a hole in his belly. Just moments later, he saw her blonde head out on the balcony, leading a man by his hand, guiding him farther into the shadows.

Shadows were her companion. The southern belle was all peaches and cream, hiding in the shadows shouldn't be so easy for her, but it was. She had moved through them like a cat and within moments, all he saw was the shadow of the man she had chosen for the night.

Now that hunger was sated, but the edgy nerves inside her weren't. They danced through her veins, energizing, but dangerous. Rafe could feel her inattention.

All around him, he could place every living creature, and knew when somebody less than human, or more than human, walked by. But he doubted Sheila was that aware.

Damn it.

An odd scent came to him on the wind. Magick. He knew the scent of magick and the feel of it, the way it could taste golden on the tongue. Or very bitter.

This was tasteless though. Sexless almost. Witch power tended to be very sexual in nature. Not sensual, but sexual. He could tell when the magick worker was man or woman, but not this time.

The magick felt immature—not young, exactly. There was an aged feeling to it, but still some sort of childlike amazement in it.

And it was *strong*.

That wasn't right. A power like that, wouldn't they have felt it before now? Wouldn't the witch have felt them? Come looking for them?

Noticed them?

That was when the sense of magick he felt focused, almost as if he had caused it. It strengthened, became more determined, almost as if it had matured in a matter of heartbeats.

All focused on Sheila.

Something about her had intensified the interest. Made that almost sleepy power sharpen and define itself.

He dodged into the alley and fell into a run, his feet slapping soundlessly against the pavement as he ran, the wind blowing into his face as he sped across the distance that separated them.

Too late...

The internal time clock in his head sounded as he heard Sheila's whispered murmur of shock, the surprise that flowed through her. There was no way he should be so aware of her. No reason he should feel the hands that closed over her arms, or feel the warm flow of breath on her face.

Flying around the corner, he hurtled down the alley where he could smell her, scent her, taste the shock within her.

His blade was in his hands. He barely remembered drawing it, but it was in his hands—deadly, menacing. Images pounded into his mind—blood flying, death... *Nobody* touched his woman.

"Get your bloody hands off of her!" he roared as he dove for the tall, dark-skinned man holding her.

"Rafe, no!" Sheila shouted.

But he heard nothing beyond the blood roaring in his ears, saw nothing beyond the sight of a man towering over his woman, holding her close to him as he stared down into her face.

His eyes lifted from Sheila's face just as Rafe reached him and he let her go, shoving her behind him. Later, Rafe would see the protectiveness of that gesture, but all he saw now was a man touching his woman.

Shifting his grip on the sword, he swung out, clipping him across the face with the pommel. But the silent giant never budged. Slowly, the man reached up, touched a hand to his high cheekbones, closed his eyes then opened them as he shook his head back and forth.

"You hit me," he murmured quietly, touching big, blunt fingers to his jaw.

"Damn it, Rafe, just like a fucking man. Always thinking with something other than your brain," Sheila snapped, forcing her body between Rafe and her new friend. "Put that damned thing away."

Rafe snarled at her and said, "So you like having a stranger put his hands all over you?"

"He wasn't putting them all over me, Rafe. Grow up," she said pithily, turning on her heel and looking up at the rather quiet man.

"Are you okay, Robbie?" she asked. Rafe's brows drew low over his eyes as he heard the soft, patient note in her voice.

Like the way she'd talk to a child.

Rafe's scowl melted away as he lifted his eyes and truly looked.

Those black eyes were blank. The air around him was all but colored with magick and Rafe could feel it beating against his mind. It was staggering, that power. He'd only met a few witches who had that intensity to their magick, that much confined power.

But the eyes he was staring into were like that of a child – petulant, angry, afraid.

Bloody hell, Rafe thought, bemused. Slowly, feeling like an idiot, he slid the sword back into its sheath while embarrassment flooded through him.

"Robbie, it's okay. He's an idiot, but he's a good guy," Sheila said.

Rafe watched as the giant's eyes dropped to rest on Sheila's face. "He hit me," he whispered.

"He thought you were going to hurt me," Sheila said quietly. "He was trying to protect me."

Rafe watched as the man looked from Sheila to him. Slowly, he nodded. "Good guys protect others," he said it as though he was repeating something he had been told many times. "No matter what it takes."

"That's right," Sheila said. "Your friend told you that?"

Confusion and disbelief tied a nasty knot in Rafe's belly. Those eyes bothered him. Like the witch's power. Immature, young...yet aged. A child caught in a man's body. Forever.

"Yes. My friend told me. She tells me lots of things," he said, nodding his head, he smiled that sweet, innocent smile.

"Take us to her," Sheila said, smiling gently. "I'd like to meet her, Robbie."

Rafe moved up closer to the quiet man, resting his hand on Sheila's shoulder.

Robbie shook his head. "I can't," he whispered, shaking his head. "She's not strong like you. I have to protect her. I was just supposed to get her something to eat. She's hungry. Doesn't eat like she should. But she hates it so."

Hates it... Rafe's instincts started to whisper and clamor inside him. "Maybe we can help," he said quietly. "I've been there before."

The man nodded. "Being a vampire is no fun," he murmured, his big shoulders slumping.

* * * * *

Whatever Sheila had been expecting, it wasn't this. Wasn't this diminutive creature who hid in the shadows as Robbie tried to coax her to come out. "They aren't bad," Robbie insisted. "Ella, please. The lady is nice. But he hit me."

"You *hit* him?" It was a young woman's voice, full of anger and fury. Sheila watched as she came rushing out of the shadows, her single eye glowing, fangs dropped as she placed her body protectively in front of Robbie. The other eye was just gone. It its place was an angry, puckered mark in the delicate oval of her face, almost lost in the long twisted scars that ran down from her forehead, slashing across one cheek.

"Sweet heaven." The words came whispered over her shoulder and she decided that Rafe was as surprised as she was.

Lifting her chin pugnaciously, she demanded, "What is wrong with you? Hitting Robbie... Do you like beating on those who are weaker than you?" She sniffed depreciatingly and snapped, "Some bloody Hunter you are."

"Rafe came at the wrong time," Sheila interrupted, sliding forward, catching the vampire's gaze. "He saw Robbie holding my arms and thought I was in trouble. He's a blockhead, but he didn't mean any harm."

Sheila could feel the dark scowl that Rafe directed at her, but she ignored it.

"Haven't you learned to look with more than your eyes?" the slight woman asked, lifting her chin imperiously.

"Ahhh…guess not," Rafe said, shrugging.

The woman studied them for a long moment and then she sighed. "Robbie, why did you bring them here?"

The smile on Robbie's face was serene, happy. "They wanted to help."

As the woman sighed, a soft, broken little sound, Sheila felt her heart break. "They can't help us, Robbie. Nobody can." She moved a little closer, looking at them as she murmured, "Not even the illustrious Hunters."

Sheila heard the bitterness in her voice and something hot and angry moved through her belly. Something bad had been done to these two. Very bad.

"You're just a kid," Sheila murmured, staring down at the fey creature. Her head barely reached Sheila's breastbone, and Sheila wasn't a tall woman. Her body was slight, slender, just the beginning of curves on her form and her face still had the softness of childhood.

A sad smile curved the vampire's lips as she shook her head. "I'm more than four hundred years old, child. I was killed when I was but a girl, but I haven't been a child for many years. My body stopped maturing, but my brain did not." She turned to the man behind her and hugged him, wrapping her arms around his waist and murmuring to him before stroking a hand down his arm. "Robbie, well, he will never be much more than a child. But he's been a good friend, helped me break free from the one who made me. Makes sure I take care of myself. And I take care of him."

One petite shoulder lifted as she said, "I'm incomplete. I never reached full power as a vampire. I was too young when he changed me. And I wasn't very strong when I was alive. Then he starved me for decades. I'll never be strong. But I'm smart. Robbie is strong, but he has a child's mind. Together we are a whole person."

Sheila felt a fist wrap around her heart as she saw the sadness in the girl's face. Robbie reached out and patted her shoulder. "We're fine," he said, smiling guilelessly. "We got away from him. And we don't have to be afraid all the time. Sometimes I can even help people."

Her name was Ella. Sheila settled down on the chair, listening as Ella relayed what had happened to her years ago. The girl—woman—was lonely. And she was a woman, but forever trapped in a body that would never see the full bloom of womanhood.

The smell of magick and blood was heavy in the air. She rubbed her nose as a familiar scent teased her nostrils.

"How long have you been here?" Rafe asked.

She slid him a glance, seeing little more than his eyes as a splash of light fell across his forehead and cheekbones, leaving all of him in shadow, save for those deep penetrating eyes. A shiver raced down her spine, but Sheila turned away from him, looking back at Ella as the vampire settled back with a thoughtful frown on her face.

"A few months, maybe," she murmured, finally shrugging. "I do not keep track of time well. But we will have to go soon. It was safe when we first came, but lately, there have been signs of others here. We cannot fight against a Master vampire and win."

Sheila cocked a brow at her. "Why are you so certain you would have to fight? Most vampires are rather peaceful."

Ella smirked. "Yes. And Hunters like you make sure it stays that way," she said, grinning as Sheila's brows rose. "A Hunter has a feel all their own. Robbie never would have brought you here if he didn't know you were safe. He felt it before I did. Regardless of his handicap, maybe because of it, he has a remarkable ability to read people."

Then she leaned forward, bracing her elbows on the table, a weary sigh escaping her. "But something else is here now. Something wrong. He kills. He hides." Her voice dropped to a ghostly whisper and fear made her eyes glow. "We are not safe here."

Ella turned away, her slight shoulders slumping. Robbie moved up to her and Sheila watched as the big man wrapped a protective arm around her, hugging her close.

Her nose twitched and she reached up, rubbing it again. Damn it, that smell, what was it…so familiar…

The knowledge hit her like a fist in the belly, sending all of the air from her lungs in a rush, spinning around, her hair flying around her shoulders as she dove for the closed door in the corner of the room. *Dominic…*

"Sheila?"

She shook her head as she shoved the door open, sending it crashing into the wall, tearing from one of the hinges so that it hung crooked. The still form lying on the bed caused tears to burn her eyes. Her ears caught the ever-so faint lub-dub of his heart.

Too slow…far too slow…

In his neck, a nasty ragged bite was healing. She saw a bandage at his elbow and suspected it hid another bite. His lashes were closed over those dark, gentle eyes. And at his upper lip…the faint bulge of fangs.

She spun around, eyes wild as she dove toward Ella. Rafe's hands caught her around her upper arms and he pinned her struggling body against his as she shouted, "What did you fucking do? He was harmless! You killed him."

The diminutive vampire shook her head, but the words coming from her fell on empty ears. It was Rafe who made her listen. His arms—so strong, and oddly gentle—wrapped around her and he lowered his head, murmuring in her ear, "Sheila…baby, she couldn't have done that. What was done to him was evil—we felt it in the air. That girl doesn't have an evil bone in her body."

The strength went out of her legs and she collapsed, feeling Rafe's arm come up under her knees and then she was cradled against his chest as tears rolled unchecked down her cheeks. "Rafe—who did it then? He's a sweet guy. Just a sweet guy…no threat to anybody."

* * * * *

He was a threat. To Rafe. A very big one now, and the jealousy in his gut was tearing him in two. But the pain, the confusion that he saw in Sheila's eyes tore at his heart.

"Belle, the feral creatures couldn't care less about any of that," he whispered, carrying her into the small bedroom, lowering himself onto the sole chair, watching as Sheila's eyes were drawn back to the still body under the sheet. He was sleeping. The deep, sound sleep of the newly changed. He would sleep close to eighteen hours a day at first. Strength came slowly to the new ones.

Almost like a newborn babe, he had to be cared for and watched, otherwise he just might fade away.

"Somebody killed him," she repeated numbly. He suspected she was remembering her own change. The man who had changed her had been her first lover, a man who had disappeared only days before they would have been married. He'd survived the change, but not with his sanity intact. Joe Gilbert had come looking for his childhood sweetheart, ten years after he had disappeared.

And Sheila had opened her door to him. Not to welcome him back into her life, but to tell him off for walking away from her.

Her death and rebirth as a vampire had been a brutal one. He knew just how brutal and ugly it must have been—her sweet, soft body had only one imperfection…a nasty, jagged bite on the curve where her neck and her shoulder met, usually hidden by the soft sweaters she wore.

Her ex-lover had beaten her when she'd recoiled in fear from him. Beaten her, mauled her, tortured her, and then he'd bitten her and forced his blood down her throat. He'd dragged her away from her home that night, but he hadn't gotten far. Kelsey was the one who'd seen the weak vampire attempting to run away from Joe Gilbert less than a day after she'd been Changed.

Needless to say, he hadn't survived that encounter.

Rafe had only seen the witch upset a time or two, but it wasn't an experience one forgot easily. Sheila had once confided in him that Kelsey had lit Joe Gilbert up like a fireball.

Some days, Rafe wished the witch had left Joe alive. Just so *he* could have the pleasure of killing the bastard himself, slowly…painfully. He'd woken up too many times with Sheila shivering in the bed next to him, fighting and struggling in her sleep.

Damn it, her pain had always torn at him.

This was no easier.

The shadows in her eyes closed a tight fist around Rafe's heart and he wished he could do something— *anything*— to take them away.

"He's not dead, pet," Rafe said finally, his voice low and hoarse. "You are right about one thing—he is a decent guy. You can see straight through him—he's strong. He'll come through this fine."

"*Not fine*," Sheila cried out, burying her face in her hands. "Damn it, he wanted to be a doctor. Wants kids. He loves sunrises and sunsets and a million other things that *we* can't have!"

"If he loves life, then he will welcome the chance he's been given," Rafe said. "It may take time…but what would you rather be? Dead? Or as you are now?"

"I *am* dead." She grabbed his hand and pressed it to her breast, and Rafe could have cursed as he felt the heat of her flesh, the silken softness of it. Her fury had warmed her blood, increased her heart rate. As he held his hand over her chest, he counted two beats as he stared into her eyes. "Do you feel that? If I was *alive*, this heart would beat more. If I was alive, I could have a family, have *something*."

"If you were dead, you wouldn't be in my arms right now, and this heart of yours, this wonderful, open, amazing heart wouldn't be beating at all," he said gently. He pulled his hand away, trailing his fingers over the soft skin of her chest before he cupped her chin. "You are alive, Sheila. As is your...lover."

The word was distasteful to him. But she cared about this kid. And Rafe was damned tired of seeing unhappiness in her clear blue eyes. If this was what she wanted...

A soft voice came from the doorway. "He is weak still. I haven't the strength to bring him back. Robbie found him, and brought him here. Together, we've kept him alive, but he has no bond, no strength inside him to make it through the change."

Rafe met the woman's eyes and saw the weariness, the bitterness there. He knew what she was asking. "You tried to feed him? Forge a bond?"

She nodded slowly as a tear trickled down her cheek. "I am not strong enough. I am no Master. My blood isn't enough for him."

Damn, the irony... Not only was he going to have to let her go...he was going to have to be the one who saved her lover. *I never should have let you push me away*, he thought bitterly as he pressed his lips to her brow.

Rising, he placed Sheila in the chair and went over to the kid's side. "Damn it, how old is he, Sheila?" he asked. In sleep, Dominic looked amazingly young. And sweet. Almost innocent.

"Twenty-two," she said thickly. "Forever."

Ella laughed. It was a cold, humorless sound and there was a wealth of knowledge in her gaze. "No. He will not be twenty-two forever. His face may stay as young and handsome as he is now...just like I will forever be caught in this hideous child's body. But the mind will continue to grow, he will live...learn. Although I do not know if I agree with your friend... Is this truly better than death?"

Rafe suspected he knew this unknown vampire's answer to that question, at least for herself. She wished for death. He could taste her bitter anger and weariness in the air. Crouching down, he stared at Dominic's face and whispered his name.

His lashes fluttered, but he stayed asleep. The gray cast of his skin bothered Rafe. Even from just a light feeding, with no bond, he should have had better color than that. Tapping the cool cheek, Rafe said, "Dominic," louder, harsher, forcing power into his words as he spoke.

This time, the lashes lifted for a brief moment and Dominic muttered groggily, "Get the hell away."

Rafe snorted. "Cocky bastard, isn't he?" He knelt down and whispered, "Do you remember what happened to you?"

Setting back on his heels, he waited as those lashes lifted again, and the man on the bed glared up at him in cold fury. "Get the fuck away from me," he rasped.

"I would say you do," he murmured, thoughtfully. Damn, the fury that had flooded the newly Changed vampire at those words...it was almost choking, it hung so thick in the air.

Good.

Anger could help a man survive a good long while—long enough to get strong. "Do you want to get your pound of flesh...or should I say, pints of blood, back?"

"Not real. It's a fucking dream, I'm sick and dreaming and none of this is happening," Dominic snarled, fire leaping into his eyes.

Sympathy moved through Rafe, because behind that fire, was fear, shame, and loathing. Something bad had been done to him, and not just the taking of blood.

"You are sick. And I imagine you've had some unpleasant dreams, but the fact is, Dominic, this is happening. And you can either lie there and deny it, and get weaker and weaker, or you can let me help you. Once you're strong, you can do something about it."

* * * * *

Sheila watched from the shadows as Rafe took Dominic's wrist and sank his teeth in. The rich musk of vampire blood filled the air, but it was...flat, somehow. Dominic truly was sick. Weak and sick. And madder than hell, from the fire shining in his eyes.

His face pinched with pain as Rafe fed for just the briefest of moments, and then Rafe used his fangs to tear his wrist open, holding it in front of Dominic's mouth. Dominic turned away, his mouth twisting in a grimace. "No choice, kid. Not if you want to ever crawl out of this bed," Rafe said flatly. "Not if you want their blood."

After a long moment passed, Dominic reached up and curled his hand around Rafe's wrist and for a second, Sheila thought he was going to refuse. But then the hunger flared in his eyes and he closed his mouth around Rafe's wrist, his jaws working greedily as he fed, eyes narrowing to slits.

Something heavy and powerful moved through the air and Sheila watched as a glow began to pulse in Rafe's eyes. She hadn't seen this before. She'd never made another vampire, and all those she had met were older than she. This was the first time she'd ever seen a vampire feed another for something other than sex.

The power swelled to a crescendo and then like a water balloon thrown against a wall, it exploded, raining down on all of them. Dominic fell back from Rafe's wrist, eyes closed, mouth slack.

"Rafe?" Sheila whispered, her voice trembling.

He looked at her with hooded eyes. "He will be fine," he said brusquely as he accepted a white square of cloth from Ella and pressed it to his sluggishly bleeding wrist. Robbie was bandaging the bloodied wound on Dominic's wrist and Rafe watched closely, his face unreadable.

"He'll need to feed when he wakes," Rafe said softly. "Something other than vampire."

"I'll bring him something," Sheila whispered, a hot, tight knot in her belly. Regret, anger...sadness? She didn't know. There was no way to put a label on the emotions running through her right now.

"I can feed him."

"Robbie, no."

Sheila and Rafe both turned to watch the petite vampire stand in front of Robbie, one hand on his sternum, as she stared up at him. "You *will not* feed him."

Robbie smiled down at Ella and patted her head, the way you would a small child, or a pet. Then he said softly, "I have to, Ella. The bad ones are too close. He needs to be strong. Witch blood is better than human blood." His voice dropped to a rough whisper as he added, "He always said that."

"He?" Sheila asked quietly, a frown puckering her forehead as she looked at Robbie. That fear again...it was hot and rancid inside Robbie, born of a torment suffered at the hands of somebody vile. She could feel his fear, all consuming, and she felt a wave of disgust at what had been done to them flow through her. What a man he could have been...strong, powerful in both magick and spirit. But he'd never be a complete man. So unfair.

Robbie nodded, his throat working as he swallowed. "Yes. The bad one. He fed from me, lots of times. Loved magick blood." A grimace twisted his face and he muttered, "About the only good thing I can do right."

"Now, Robbie, that's not true," Ella argued, shaking her head so that her silvery blonde hair floated around her shoulders. "You do a great many things well."

He frowned and said, "Not without help. I'm stupid. Can't do anything without you to remind me how. At least, this, I know I can do right. And I'm going to."

Without saying another word, he moved past Ella and Rafe, pausing by Sheila. "I'll do this. It will help."

She forced a smile and said thickly, "Yes. It will."

The gentle giant was gone, on silent feet, his big shoulders slumped, head downcast.

Ella turned around and shook her head at them. "No. I won't let him do it. Damn it, he has been used enough in his life — "

Rafe interrupted, his voice low, commanding. "Let him be a man, Ella. There is not much he can do. Surely you can understand how frustrating this can be for him. Do you think he doesn't know what he is? What he can do, he should be allowed. Give him some pride, at least."

Ella snapped out, "Pride? Feeding monsters like us is something to be proud of?"

"No. Making a decision to help somebody and following through, that is something to be proud of," Rafe replied levelly, folding his arms across his chest. With a raised brow, he said, "He is still a man. His mind never completely matured, and I realize he isn't a wunderkind. But he is still a man. He has a man's heart, and a man's soul."

To that, Ella had no response.

Rafe stared at her for a moment longer and then he walked way

Sheila moved to Dominic's side, lowering herself until she could prop her hip on the edge of the narrow bed. She heard Ella behind her, but she had nothing to say. She wasn't a monster. She wasn't pleased with what she was, but she wasn't a monster.

With a hesitant finger, she trailed her finger down her neck, feeling the raised ridge of the nasty bite there. Few vampires scarred with their sire mark, but she had—he had bit her once, shaking her like a dog would shake a plastic bone, toying with her, before he had bitten her and drank of her blood.

Dominic had suffered as well. She could feel it...Rafe had sensed something inside Dominic, and through Rafe, she felt the echo of something awful. What had they done to him?

His face was still, but no longer gray and gaunt. Behind his eyelids, she could see his eyes moving back and forth, and as she rested her hand on his chest, she felt the slow rhythm of his heart. *I'm so sorry*, she thought weakly. *I don't know why this happened to you, but I'm so sorry.*

"Are you sure this was the right thing to do? We are nothing but animals."

Sheila closed her eyes, frustrated with Ella, but pity moved within her heart as well. "No. We are what we make ourselves, Ella. The man who did this is less than an animal—he is a true monster. But I'm no monster. You aren't a monster…Rafe isn't…the people who trained me aren't monsters," she finally said. "You make your choices in this form of life, just like you did when you were human. And you will have to live with them…which means if you try to stop a good man from helping somebody helpless and weak, then you will sooner or later have to explain why."

"We are abominations," Ella said, shaking her head, tears rolling down her face. "An affront to God."

With a growl, Sheila shot to her feet, spinning around as she jerked the neckline of her shirt aside. "Look at this!" she snapped, moving her hair aside. "Do you see that? I suspect the man who changed you was no better than the one who made me. They are the monsters—*I* was a victim. *You* were a victim. I'm a damned Hunter…I save lives. I make a difference. I am no damned abomination."

"We shouldn't have survived!" Ella shouted.

Bending down and putting her face close to Ella's, she snapped, "Then we would not have. If God wanted us dead, do you think for a damned minute that any power on this earth could stop Him?"

Tears spilled down her cheeks. "It is not that simple," she whispered.

Sheila turned away, shaking her head, shoving her hands through her hair, frustrated, she sat back down by Dominic and took his hand. "It is that simple, Ella. Life *can* be black and white."

* * * * *

In the depths of the old plantation house, Pierre stalked the halls, swearing under his breath, full of frustration and rage.

His strength had yet to return to him fully.

That damned bastard Malachi, the witches—one day, though. One day he would be back to the powerful creature he had once been, and he'd hunt them down, stalk them like the sheep they were, and kill them.

All of them.

Especially that witch-bitch of Malachi's.

Oh, he knew what Malachi had done.

That tawny-skinned creature had laughed at him, even though she had known she would die. He had heard her silent laughter as he'd fed on her, whispering into her mind.

But his voice hadn't caused fear.

She had laughed. And taunted him in a strong, steady mental voice. *They will kill you. I don't care if I die or not, so long as they live…because they will have your ass.*

She should have died, in fear, in pain.

But she had lived. Malachi, the noble Hunter who never Changed a mortal, had brought her over and saved her life.

Now she was one of the most deadly creatures on earth.

Both witch and vampire. Like Pierre. But as a mortal, Pierre hadn't been that strong a witch. She was. Strong…very strong…

It had been more than a year since that night and he had yet to regain his strength. And before he could finish off that rather handsome young man in the alley, something had come.

A light—brilliant and as strong as the sun—had flooded the alley and from it, a man had walked out.

Pierre had flung an arm over his face and in the moment that he had hidden from the light, panicked, the man had come, taken Pierre's new toy, and disappeared.

This was the third time someone in this city had robbed him of his prey. It wasn't a Hunter. He'd have known. And a Hunter wouldn't just take his prey — a Hunter would try to kill him. Try to Hunt him.

Try.

But until tonight, nobody had even made an attempt.

The magick that had come snaking out of the dark had been like an assassin's blade, sure, certain and deadly. Looking for him.

It had found him as well, and retreated, before Pierre had even had a chance to send his own magick out to find the spellcaster. Pierre was an accomplished witch, with a great deal of power to his call.

But he could only do so much. He had the power, but not the skill. Skill was something a witch leveled out on, and he had hit his peak long ago. Learning different magicks, different spells had given him an edge, but there was only so much for him to learn.

Whoever this unknown witch was, he or she was his match.

For a moment, he cursed that Indian bastard who had gotten away from him decades ago. His scarred little pet had befriended that freak and together, they had run away, and stayed hidden a very long time. Pierre had long since given up searching for his witch. But, through him, Pierre had been able to accomplish bigger magicks, and he'd had an untapped fount of skill and power.

So far, none of the witches he'd taken had been equal. Now that little wolf-witch might have been a match, and then Malachi's witch-bitch. Pierre shouldn't have drained her without forcing some of his own blood down her golden throat. She would have been his then, and he'd once more have had access to the more powerful magicks.

And he'd be able to figure out who had been tracking him now.

It wasn't the Hunter witch. The red-haired woman who still looked to be a girl. She lived here, or she had once. But she never came through here—at least not since Pierre had been trolling in Memphis.

The first two years, it had been silent, the lesser vampires and weres leaving as Pierre's net of power had spread across the city. But then that unknown witch had come the first time, saving a young woman, no more than girl really, before Pierre had even had a chance to break her lily-white skin.

Then a pretty little boy witch, just barely out of his teens. It hadn't been light that time. It had been fire.

Or the illusion of it, at least. Convincing enough that Pierre had flinched away from it. And then the man had come, taken the witch, and disappeared into the night while Pierre summoned a spell against the fire.

The fire had died with the unknown witch's leaving, though, which left Pierre to wonder if the fire had existed, or if he had just thought it did.

Who was he? Never had Pierre seen his face—the man moved through shadows like a panther, swift and silent.

"*Merde.*"

"Master?"

The slave who spoke from the shadows cowered as she rose from the floor, her eyes rapt on his face, full of fear, full of devotion. "Nothing," he spat at her, turning away from her. Stalking to the window, he jerked open the heavy drapes, staring out into the night.

As if losing his prey wasn't enough, now he had something else to deal with. The unknown witch.

And a new vampire in town.

Pierre had felt the presence days ago, but ignored it. Eventually, all the vampires fled from him, without even knowing why. The aura of fear he emanated saw to that.

But this vampire hadn't fled.

Whoever it was, this new vampire not only wasn't worried—he was trolling. Not for prey, though. Pierre would know if another vampire was hunting for prey on *his* land.

No. This vampire was searching for something…a monster…maybe even Pierre himself.

Then that spell…

When had such a powerful witch arrived? Pierre should have felt the witch's arrival. And why in the hell couldn't he find the witch who was stealing his toys away before he even had a chance to really play?

Could they be one and the same? Was this witch a creature like himself, one who could cloak himself from prying eyes? That would explain why Pierre hadn't felt the witch's arrival. Or perhaps the witch had even been here first…*yes*.

The same…the thought hadn't occurred to him before. A witch powerful enough to face him, to steal his prey, he should have felt such a presence. But if the witch could cloak himself…

The rage tore through him and he whirled, grabbing the quiet little slave and jerking her upward, lifting his arm and backhanding her. As she crumpled, he perked up a little, smiling at the rush of fear and pain that flooded the air. That was a little better. He slid his hand down and cupped her cunt, digging his fingers inside her. Even as she flinched in pain, she reached for him, and as Pierre let her wrap her arms around him, he kissed her, biting her lip.

The blood that flooded his mouth was flat, almost tasteless, but the tang of her fear and hunger added some spice.

He'd drained her too close. Fed her too much of his own.

She just wasn't much fun anymore.

It was time for a new pet—one with a little stronger willpower. Once they broke, they just didn't bring any pleasure.

Chapter Five

The ceiling overhead was gray, dank. Like he was underground. That would explain why in the hell he was so cold.

Dominic had long since lost track of where he was, how long he'd been there. Nothing seemed real.

Not that guy —

Dominic shut that out of his mind. Hadn't happened. Whatever nasty dreams lurked in his sleep were just dreams — not memories. It hadn't happened.

God — closing his eyes tightly, he flung an arm over his face, trying to block out whatever it was in his mind, whatever had happened... It lurked on the edge of his mind, like a forgotten song, almost there, just out of reach. But not far enough. It was still so close.

Not far enough.

The horrid pain in his neck was finally fading away. It had been more like a low-level toothache for days, but before that, it had been obscene in its intensity.

Now it was all but gone. And when he touched his neck, the ragged flesh felt smoother, like it was healing.

Thinking of the pain made memories flow through his mind again. Damn it, why couldn't he just stop thinking about it?

The ceiling. Dominic stared at the ceiling. If he could just focus on the ceiling, stare at it long enough, hard enough, he'd zone out again, slide back into sleep, and maybe, just maybe he could dream sweet dreams again.

* * * * *

Rafe felt Dominic waken.

Crouched in the trees, he stared at the lights in the distance, sighing as he felt Sheila move toward Dominic.

Until Dominic learned to shield a little bit, Rafe would have to block him out, otherwise he would feel every damned thought that moved through his head. And Sheila...he was so acutely attuned to her that he had to concentrate to block her out of his head.

And he didn't want to be linked with her while she was near Dominic. Hell, if Dominic was within a hundred-mile radius, he didn't really want to be around. But he had eliminated any chance of that, the minute he'd used his strength to bond Dominic as he'd worked through the change.

Slamming his shielding down, he rose and started back down the trail that led to Ella and Robbie's home. Hunger growled and rumbled in his belly but it wasn't his. It was the echo from Dominic.

The moment he stepped through the door, he felt Robbie's eyes on him. Saw the nerves and worry there. Arching a brow, he said softly, "You don't have to do this."

"I think I do." Robbie's dark eyes looked just a little more...normal, Rafe decided as he stared into them and felt the witch's resolve.

Ella huddled in the corner, her expression troubled and dark. "You do not have to," Ella whispered. "Why do you think you have to do it? They'll find him something,

Robbie. It doesn't have to be you. You saved him already. You owe him nothing. You don't have to do this for him."

"I have to do it for me," Robbie said quietly. He swallowed, shaking his head. "I don't want to be afraid all the time." His eyes moved to Rafe, and Rafe felt a terrible rage burn through him at the fear in Robbie's eyes. "He was bad, the man who made Ella, the one who locked me up all the time, starved me, beat me, if I didn't do what he wanted. He made me afraid. I never used to be afraid."

His eyes closed and those big shoulders drooped for a moment as he whispered, "I'm tired of being afraid." He sounded more like a child than a creature who had walked the earth for decades, if not centuries.

A surge of resentment flooded Rafe as he moved aside and let Robbie approach Dominic. That was one hell of a man—he had the heart of a man, the pride of a man, locked forever inside the mind of a kid.

Sometimes, life really sucked.

As if to echo that thought, he felt Sheila moving up behind him. The scent of her filled his head, and he felt that hunger for her awaken. His cock ached, his heart ached, his hands ached... ached to hold her, touch her, make her love him again.

She had, once. He'd killed it, and now he had lost her.

Rafe shoved the emotions aside, shrugging out of his coat, tossing it on the table before reaching for the blade at his spine. Laying the blade atop his coat, he turned and studied Dominic.

Crossing to him, Rafe said softly, "How do you feel?"

"Like I'm dead." The words were flat, empty and cold.

Rafe cracked a grin. "You aren't. I can promise you that."

Robbie moved out of the shadows slowly, pausing to look at Rafe. Rafe smiled tightly. "It's okay, Robbie. Go ahead."

Dominic jerked his eyes to Robbie as the witch moved up to the bed, kneeling beside him. "You need to feed. A heavy feeding, from somebody truly alive—Robbie said he'd feed you," Rafe said quietly.

"I don't want to feed," Dominic muttered, turning his head to the wall and closing his eyes.

"If you don't feed, you'll stay weak," Sheila murmured.

"What the fuck does it matter?"

His voice was weary, despondent. Rafe sighed, shoving a hand through his hair before moving to stand over the bed. "You just want to lie there? Whipped? He wins, that way. You can lie there, and let him get away with it. Or you can get stronger. When you're stronger, you can join us and help us stop men like him from doing this to others."

No response.

Sheila tried to force a smile and Rafe felt his heart clench at the pain in her eyes. "Dominic, it will be okay. This... I know this has changed things for you, but that doesn't have to be bad."

Sheila flinched as Dominic turned his head and stared at her. The black, burning gaze was so full of fury, Rafe automatically moved to stand protectively in front of Sheila, flashing his fangs at Dominic.

"You don't know *anything*," Dominic snarled, ignoring Rafe as he sat up slowly, swinging his legs around and planting his feet on the floor as he used his hands to brace his weight. "*Nothing*." Jabbing a thumb to the healing gash on his neck, he snapped, "You really think being made into some sort of freak is what I'm pissed about? You don't know what they did."

Rafe turned around as Sheila gasped softly and wrapped his arms around her, lowering his head to murmur in her ear. "Easy, pet," he whispered, stroking his hand up and down her back in a soothing motion as he watched two tears, diamond-bright, trickle down her smooth cheeks.

Her hands came up to his waist and she squeezed him gently, forcing a smile. "I think maybe I should go. I'm not helping." She moved back and turned around, walking away with her shoulders slumped. She paused in the doorway and without turning back, she whispered, "I think I understand better than you realize, Dominic."

Rafe said nothing as he listened to the soft fall of Sheila's footsteps. Once she had left, he turned and looked at Dominic with cool eyes that hid the hot fury that moved through him. That wounded look in her eyes had infuriated him.

"I'm going to make a few exceptions—normally, I'd tear apart somebody who put that kind of pain in her eyes. But you've had a rough time lately, so you get a free pass. Don't do it again."

Dominic's lip lifted in a sneer and he said, "I don't need little Miss Sunshine murmuring platitudes to me. The party girl doesn't know shit about what I went through."

Rafe cocked a brow. "They raped you. You think you're the first man they've done it to?" he asked bluntly. "That party girl was changed by a man she loved. They were going to be married and then he disappeared. Somebody bit him and Changed him, and ten years later, he came back after Sheila. Only he wasn't the boy she'd loved. Wasn't even a man, really. The Change had turned him into an animal. A monster. Any idea what a vampire can do to a human woman? He tore her apart."

Dominic's eyes fell away but Rafe wasn't mollified. "I can't say I've ever been where you are," he said flatly. "I do know that if I was, I wouldn't be happy until I killed the bastards.

"Sheila *has* been where you are. But it was worse for her, because the people who did this to you—they were strangers. I know. I know what they did, what they look like—every time you think of them, every time you close your eyes you're stuck there again, and I feel it. But Sheila knew the man who raped her, who beat her, who Changed her. And her Change was *brutal*. She loved him, and then he turned into a monster and almost killed her."

"I didn't know." Dominic turned his head away and Rafe felt the impotent fury, the grief inside him.

"Doesn't matter. You hurt her. When you've been hurt, you do what a lot of people do, you strike out. You struck out at her—you hurt her, you wanted to. You do it again, I'll rip you to shreds. And you won't get the chance to help us track down the men who did this. You won't get the chance to see their blood flow. Because I'll kill you."

Through all of this, Robbie remained silent, sitting on the floor and waiting patiently. But now he spoke up, his voice quiet as he said, "He's a bad man. He likes to hurt people."

Something in Robbie's voice had Rafe shifting his gaze, wondering. "You know him, Robbie?"

The big man nodded his head, staring at the floor. "I felt his touch. It's all over Dominic. Ella recognized his smell. I know his touch. He's the bad man."

"The one who Changed Ella?" Rafe asked. "Locked you up?"

The witch nodded and he reached up, touching the bite on Dominic's neck. Dom flinched and Robbie jerked his hand back, his face going blank and smooth as a doll's.

"He likes to hurt people. He's good at it. Been doing it a long time. Me and Ella, we were going to leave the night we found Dominic. Knew he was close. He's been close, but we hoped he'd move. He's not though, so we got to run, stay away from him. But we didn't want to let him kill anybody else."

Dominic laughed bitterly. "Appreciate the thought, but you were a little too late. He *did* kill me."

Rafe shook his head. "No. He Changed you. There is life inside you still, just a different kind of life. You aren't dead. You're just not human anymore." Rafe moved to crouch on the floor by Robbie, smiling as Robbie turned his head to stare at him. "Do you know his name, Robbie? I can stop him—if you can help me."

"Pierre. His name is Pierre," Robbie whispered, eyes dark and haunted. "But he's not just a vampire. He's got magick—he's a bad man. Bad, bad, bad…"

* * * * *

Rafe shoved a hand through his hair as he prowled the small confines of the room hours later. Dominic had finally agreed to feed, and now he was sleeping. Robbie had done something, because the new vampire was sleeping dreamlessly, and for the first time since he'd fed Dominic, Rafe only had his own thoughts in his head.

Pierre.

The name wasn't unknown to him.

The bastard had bitten the witch Leandra, nearly killed her. Would have if Malachi hadn't brought her over. Malachi didn't sire people—but he'd brought her over. Now he trained her, but they had yet to catch the man responsible.

Malachi had put the word out that if Pierre was found, he wanted him.

Rafe suspected he wanted Pierre for Leandra, so she could settle her score with him. But Pierre was *here*.

And something inside of Rafe rebelled at the thought of turning this problem over to another. His land... Fury shot through him, fury, possessiveness, emotions he couldn't even explain as he thought of Malachi coming here.

Any Master would be bad...but Malachi, fuck, he'd be even worse.

He didn't want the ancient one on his land.

He stilled as the thought passed through his head. His land. His territory. Like the missing piece of the puzzle, that one thought made everything that had been biting at him over the past few months fall into place.

His aggression, his rampant bursts of fury, how he had come to resent Eli, even as he'd sought his Master's approval.

Rafe had become a Master. It wasn't an unexpected thing—Eli had told him, decades ago, he had the mark of a

Master inside him and he'd become one, provided he lived long enough.

He'd suspected he'd get there in time. Knew sooner or later that he'd probably leave Eli's enclave and start his own, but he hadn't expected it to be an actual physical ache within him, hadn't expected he'd need his own space so soon. Hadn't expected this deep possessiveness... Hadn't expected it to happen so soon.

Or thought about what it meant...leaving Sheila.

Not that she was his anymore.

But to be someplace hundreds of miles away from her — where he couldn't see her smile, hear that soft laugh, smell the soft scent of her skin.

But it was inevitable. Irrefutable.

He had found his territory and it was here. It was his responsibility to deal with the monster who was preying within his land.

* * * * *

Sheila came inside just in time to see Rafe rising from his crouch on the floor. He'd been staring into the fire and she shivered at the fury she saw flickering in his eyes. Fury wasn't an unknown emotion for Rafe. His emotions were like quicksilver, always burning hot, and quick to spill over.

What she saw in his eyes, though, was different.

It was fury.

But there was control there now. There were times when she doubted Rafe knew what control was. But his fury now was tightly reined in, controlled, laser-sharp instead of burning like a forest fire.

"Rafe?" She kept her voice level. Any sign of nervousness from her in the past had always called out to a demon inside of Rafe, and she knew better than to show any sign of weakness in front of him until she knew what had set him off.

"Are you okay?" he asked neutrally.

She moved her shoulders in a restless shrug. "Dom's confused. Hurt. Angry." Sheila poked her lip out, sulking a little as she added, "I can't say it didn't hurt, but I understand how he feels. A little, at least." Cocking her head, she studied him. "What's going on in that head of yours, Rafe?"

A small, humorless smile curved his lips. "A hundred different things, Belle." His gaze turned dark and he moved closer, looming over her.

She trembled as his hand came up and cupped her face. It had been too long…that simple touch set her blood to singing and turned her insides to lava. Closing her eyes, she fought to leash her hunger before he saw it.

Her mouth buzzed as he stroked his thumb over the lower curve of her lip. "I want you to leave Memphis. Take Dominic and the others with you, go to back to Eli."

Sheila's eyes flew open and she stared up at him as she said, "Leave?" Slowly, she backed away from him, watching as his hand fell to his side, fingers curling into a fist for a brief second. "No. I'm not leaving, pal," she said, shaking her head. "Too much is going on here."

"And I don't want you involved in it," Rafe said bluntly, his eyes narrowed on her face.

"Don't want me involved in it? Um, excuse me, but last I checked I was still a Hunter. And you can't exactly tell me what to do," she said on a huff, turning around as she slid her jacket off her shoulders and hung it on the peg by the door.

She jumped as he murmured into her ear, "Now that is where you are wrong. This is my problem, my fight, so get out."

Spinning around, she glared up at him, hands planted on her hips, lifting her chin. "Make me," she taunted.

His fingers closed over her chin and Sheila tried to jerk back as he leaned down and growled, "Don't push me, pet. You know how much that turns me on."

Sheila only lifted a brow, even though her heart started to slam against her ribs. Fighting had practically been foreplay for them, and she could feel the heat flowing from his body. Vampires were cool creatures. Heat came with hunger, with lust, with anger.

And judging by the hooded look in his eyes, he was hungry, all right. But it wasn't a physical appetite that he wanted to satisfy. She forced herself to shrug, keeping a disinterested look on her face as she replied, "I'm staying, Rafe."

"No."

"Oh, go soak your head, slick. I've got just as much right to be here as you do. More. Dominic was my responsibility—"

"No. He's mine. This is *my* land, and when somebody in my land is threatened, I handle it," he said authoritatively.

His words echoed in her head for the longest time before they finally made sense. *His* land. "Your land," she murmured. "You certain about that, slick?"

He gave a short, terse nod as he said, "Yes. I've felt edgy since I got here, and I finally figured out why. This is *my* land, babe. I'll deal with it. Go to Eli."

Sheila laughed, shaking her head. "I know the rules, *babe*. I was here before you claimed your territory. I've been living here for a while. Set up residence and everything. And I don't want to leave. So if you insist on me leaving, you're going to have to make me." Lifting her chin pugnaciously, she drawled, "So, you wanna fight it out?"

* * * * *

When she lifted that chin and glared at him down the length of her cute little up-turned nose, all Rafe wanted to do was turn her over his knee and spank her. Damn it, this was *serious*. And she was snickering at him and daring him to make her leave.

The hard truth was, though, if he wanted to make her leave, and she refused, the only lawful way to do it was for them to fight it out. And he couldn't raise a hand to her.

If she was his, under his command, a member of his enclave, he could force her to leave. Once she'd sworn an oath, she was bound to uphold it. But she was Eli's.

And he'd bet his next sunset that Eli wouldn't do a damn thing that Rafe requested of him. Not right now. Eli was still too mad at him. Hell, most of them were. Sarel wasn't happy with him, Lori wasn't happy with him. Even Jonathan had told him he was being a bastard.

"Sheila, go home," he repeated.

She smiled angelically at him and said, "I am home."

With a growl, he cupped his hand over the back of her neck and jerked her against him, slanting his mouth across hers. *Safe.* He just wanted her safe. Hungrily, he pushed his tongue inside the sweet well of her mouth, gorging on her taste.

Her hands slid up his chest and she rose onto her toes, arching against him. Through the soft knit of her sweater, he felt her nipples stab into his chest and he pulled back, grabbing the hem of her sweater and jerking it over her head. The rose-colored lace of her bra cupped her breasts, the deeper pink of her nipples almost spilling over the edge of the bra.

Pulling her back against him, he lifted her and turned, taking two steps to the table and laying her down on it. Bending over her, he plowed his fingers through her hair, arching her face up to his and taking her mouth again. "I want you," he growled. "Every damn day, every second of every day, all the time. You're in my head, my soul, my blood."

Her teeth caught his lip and then she licked at his mouth as Rafe pumped his hips against the covered mound of her sex. Trailing one hand down her hip, he caught the hem of her skirt and lifted it. Damn, he loved her in a skirt, all those sweet curves just waiting for his touch.

Shifting, he nuzzled through the dense blonde curls to run his lips along the exposed line of her neck. Just under the fragile shield of her skin, he could smell her — vanilla, sex and Sheila — that unique scent that was hers alone.

He found the narrow strip of silk at her hips and muttered, "You're wearing underwear. I don't like it when you wear underwear."

A weak laugh escaped her. "I didn't know it was an issue — we're not together anymore."

Rafe scowled and pushed up, bracing his weight on his elbows as he glared down at her. Nudging against her cleft, he said, "I don't think you get much more *together* than this. Well, maybe a little." Then he shoved her skirt to her waist and stripped the silky thong down her legs.

With one hand on the inside of each knee, he pushed her thighs apart, staring down at the smooth lips of her pussy. He dropped to his knees and pulled her forward so that her hips were at the edge of the table. Licking his lips, he breathed in the scent of her aroused body before he lowered his head and pressed his mouth against her.

The taste of her, spicy and sweet, exploded in his mouth as he parted her flesh and fucked his tongue in and out of her sheath. Her fingers fisted in his hair and he growled against her.

Mine. She was his. Just like this land was his. And he'd be damned if he walked away from her because she thought she wanted some young kid who barely knew how to use his dick. Lifting his head, he stared up the length of her body as he yanked his shirt off. "You're mine, pet, you know that?" he whispered as he stood.

With harsh tugs, he opened his belt and unsnapped the buttons at his fly and watched her face as her lids slowly opened. A smile appeared on her lips as she stared up at him—that slow, feline smile that drove him crazy. Her voice was low, unsteady, almost drugged-sounding, as she replied, "Hell, I knew I was yours from the get-go. You're the one who didn't want me."

Shoving his jeans down, he crawled on the table and mounted her, wedging his thighs between hers and cuddling his cock against her dewy folds. "Dominic is over," he whispered, lowering his head and catching the fleshy lobe of her ear in his teeth, biting gently.

Sheila chuckled and slid her hands up his arms, over his shoulders, then laced her fingers behind his neck. "Aren't you done talking yet? All you had to do was look at me the right way and I'd give in," she whispered. "But you just walked away from me."

Groaning, Rafe wrapped his arms around her and held her tightly against him, shifting his hips and pushing slowly inside. The silken grip of her pussy closed over him like a wet fist—tight, hot, pure ecstasy.

"I love you," he whispered as he slid deeper inside her. "I didn't want to. Didn't want to feel anything again, but you made me."

A startled gasp escaped and he lifted his head, staring into her sky-blue eyes as a tear slid from the corner of her eye. Lowering his lips to her face, he licked it away and whispered, "Ah, baby, don't cry. Please."

"Do you mean it?" she demanded, her nails biting into his flesh as she pushed against his chest and made him look at her. "Do you?"

His mouth crooked into a wry grin. "Belle, if I didn't mean it, why in the hell do you think I came looking for you?" The snug muscles in her pussy convulsed around his aching sex and a shudder racked his body as he pulled out and surged back inside.

Sheila's pelvis rose to meet his and he caught her hip in his hand, holding her still. Impaling her completely, he rotated his hips and watched as her lashes fluttered down. Rafe lowered his head and raked her neck with his teeth, watching as a thin line of blood welled where his razor-sharp incisors had grazed her skin.

Her body arched under his as he lowered his head and licked her neck, lapping the wine of her blood away with slow, thorough deliberation. Closing his mouth over the small injury, he drank from her as he fucked her. She screamed and the sound rippled down his spine, heat exploding through his veins.

The small wound was already healing as he lifted his head, pulling back to stare into her eyes. "You're delicious, Belle," he muttered, his head spinning. He felt drunk. The taste of her always hit him like a fifth of whiskey, making his head spin, his blood heat.

Sheila whimpered under him and threw her head back, screaming out his name as she drew her legs up. He felt her heels pressed into the small of his back as she wrapped her thighs around him.

Hs cock sank deeper and he braced his hands on the table beside her head, the rhythm of his hips picking up as he pummeled her. The silken tissues of her pussy seemed to suck him in, clinging to him as he pulled out, resisting his entry as he sank back inside.

Sheila lifted up and pressed her mouth to his chest, her tongue sliding out to dance over his flesh. Her nails scraped against the small circles of his nipples and Rafe groaned, the sensation as hot and intense as if she had closed her hand over his balls.

The need to come wasn't something he could fight. Dropping his weight down on top of her, he caught her face in his hands and slanted his mouth across hers, plunging his tongue inside the sweet recesses and gorging on her taste. Her tongue pushed into his mouth and he bit down gently, feeling her arch against him, the tight, diamond-hard beads of her nipples stabbing into his chest.

Sheila screamed into his mouth and Rafe felt the hot punch of satisfaction flow through his veins as she started to come around his dick—hot, tight little caresses all up and down his length as she pumped her hips against him. He burrowed inside her, burying his cock to the balls, his entire body shaking as she convulsed and shook beneath him.

He exploded inside her, his cock jerking as he came. Riding it to the end, he pulled out just a little and surged back inside her just as her body went limp. Collapsing against her, he rested his head between the sweet, plump mounds of her breasts, cupping one in his hand, just so he could feel her skin against his palm.

Against his cheek, he felt the steady, quick beat of her heart and he grinned. "Your heart's pounding away there, Belle," he murmured.

He heard the smile in her voice as she said, "I bet. If I was still human, I'd have had a heart attack already."

Turning his head, he pressed his mouth to her chest, feeling the pulse of her heart against his lips. "I adore you," he whispered.

Her breath tripped and he looked up, seeing tears gleaming in her eyes. With a half-grin, he shrugged, shifting around until he could lie beside her and catch one of those diamond-bright tears as it slid down her cheek. He licked the tiny, salty drop off his finger and then traced the damp tip in a slow circle on her breastbone.

"You're the only one who didn't know," he murmured. "I thought that I hid so well. I couldn't admit it to myself, but everybody else knew. Everybody except you."

Her arms came up and he let her push him onto his back, wrapping his arms around her as she sprawled on top of him. "You're such a jerk," she whispered huskily.

Burying his face in the golden, downy softness of her curls, he chuckled. "You keep telling me that."

She sniffled. "It's true. You *are* a jerk. I was miserable, damn it."

His heart tightened painfully in his chest and he murmured, "I'm sorry, pet. I thought I was protecting you."

She harrumphed and he had to fight a smile as she pushed herself into a sitting position, crossing her arms over those glorious tits, scowling down at him. Tipping her nose into the air, she said regally, "I don't need protection, babe."

Pushing on his hand, he sat up, watching her as he somberly agreed, "Of course not."

Then she poked her lip out and said, "Protecting me from what?"

Shifting his weight, he moved closer, kneeling in front of her as he shrugged. Laying his palms on her smooth, shapely thighs, he rubbed them with restless strokes. How could he explain it?

"I didn't think I could love anybody, pet. Ever. But I liked you, cared about you. Wanted you like crazy. Still do. I didn't want to hurt you when you started wanting more." Sliding her a narrow look from under his lashes, he added, "Did it anyway. What good was it, trying to protect you?"

Her eyes seemed to soften for a second, but then her fingers grabbed at his chest hair and she pulled sharply. Rafe yelped and clapped a hand over his chest, rubbing at the injured spot, as he glared at her. Sheila sniffed and said, "You men. You think, and you're dangerous. Either that, or more stupid than normal."

She slept the day through with Rafe lying behind her on the narrow cot, feeling the slow, irregular beat of his heart even in her sleep. When Sheila awoke, it was with a smile on her lips. Rolling over, she saw him sitting on the floor, staring at her with those dark eyes.

"You're so damned beautiful," he murmured.

She smiled, but it was a tight, strained smile. There was something in the air...tension radiating from him. It made her uneasy and she sat up slowly, automatically bringing the sheet with her and throwing it over her shoulders. "What's wrong, Rafe?" she asked quietly.

A soft sigh slid from him as he reached up, threading his fingers through her hair. Her gut clenched as she started to worry he was already sorry.

"No." Her eyes widened as he repeated it again, shifting onto his knees while he pressed his lips to her forehead. "I'm not sorry—never will be, pet," he whispered and she felt the movement of his lips against her flesh as he spoke. As he settled back on his heels, he met her stare levelly and she watched as one big, muscled shoulder lifted in a shrug. "I can feel you inside me—have for a while. Always aware of you. I knew you were in Memphis, even before I saw you. I felt you. And the closer I get to you, the more aware of you I am. Thoughts, feelings...everything."

Lowering her brows over her eyes, she glared at him. "That doesn't seem very fair," she said truculently. Her mouth turned down in a frown as she added, "Especially since I never know a damn thing going on inside in *your* head."

Rafe smiled lightly and shrugged. "You know more than anybody else does. Not even Eli ever had much luck penetrating my thick skull, as he so politely put it. But you, you've always been able to tell when I'm mad, when I'm tired…" Flashing her a wicked grin, he whispered, "When I'm…*hungry*."

Now that was true enough. At times, his emotions had swamped her. "And when you're thinking too hard," she muttered. "What's going on in that thick head of yours, Rafe? Why are you strung tight enough to break?"

"I want you to go back to the enclave."

Her spine went rigid. Coolly, she said, "No."

"Damn it, Sheila," he snarled, rising off the floor in one fluid motion. He paced the small room, shooting angry glances her way. "Listen to me—I don't want you…or them where you could get hurt."

The fear she saw in his eyes had her heart clenching. "I understand that, Rafe," she said calmly. "But you don't get it. If anything happens to you, I'm dead inside. I can't just walk away. You don't even know what it is you're facing. You're strong. But this…this monster, he's ancient. I feel it in the air. And he's more than a vampire. I won't let you face it alone."

"Damn it, Sheila, this isn't some punk kid on a crime spree. You can handle those. This is a fucking monster. You haven't faced the kind of monsters I've faced," Rafe snapped, spinning around and glaring at her. "You've never fought against one of our kind. I have. You are too…"

A golden brow winged up as his voice trailed away. "Too soft?" she supplied. "Not tough enough?"

Rising from the bed, she advanced on him, letting the sheet fall to the floor. His eyes dropped, for one brief second, to her breasts and she felt her nipples tighten under that look. Squashing down the hunger that rose, she jabbed at his chest with her finger as she snapped, "I'm *not* soft. I won't ever be a Master, damn it, but I *am* a vampire. I'm a Hunter. And I'm a decent one, too. I may not be Sarel, or Tori, or even Lori, but damn it, I *am* a Hunter and I can damn well fight."

"What about them?"

The soft question had her deflating and she turned away, burying her face in her hands. "Don't, Rafe. Don't ask me to walk away from you," she whispered thickly. There was a nagging fear in her gut that if she walked away from him now, she might never see him again.

"They need to be safe, Belle," Rafe whispered. He moved up behind, brushing her hair aside and pressing a kiss to the nape of her neck. "Ella and Robbie have never been safe. They need to know that they are. And your friend is still weak."

There was an odd note in his voice as he said *your friend*. But she couldn't figure out what. Well, other than the fact that Rafe had found her having sex with Dominic. But that had been about hunger. Nothing more. Shoving it aside, she folded her arms around her, rocking herself slightly. "Don't," she repeated, shaking her head. If he pushed...

"*No.*"

That low, angry voice might have sounded like the petulant voice of a child, but as Ella came storming through the door, the anger on her face was that of a woman, hot and furious and strong.

Sheila jumped as the door slammed into the wall, her eyes locked on Ella's scarred face. The puckered scar around her eye seemed red, almost angry, and there was fire in her gaze as she stared at them.

Sheila barely even registered that Robbie had slid into the room until she felt his hands on her shoulders, so caught up in the fury she saw on Ella's face that she was blind to everything else. But then she felt Robbie's hands on her shoulders, and the smooth cotton of the sheet as he draped it around her. She flushed, but he never even looked at her.

Robbie's eyes were all for Ella.

Sheila had never expected reinforcements coming from this corner—not from Ella. Robbie, maybe—inside that child's mind lurked the heart of a hero. But Ella...not from Ella.

Rafe moved behind her, silent, his gaze brooding as he stared at the two people in front of them. Fury, frustration...and an odd kind of pride, all tangled inside them as he watched the witch with the vampire.

Robbie laid one big hand on Ella's face and asked, "You understand now, don't you?"

It was the most grown-up he had ever sounded, Rafe suspected. As Ella stared up at Robbie, there was a flicker of surprise in her gaze as she nodded. "I do, Robbie. You knew before I did."

Robbie smiled, a young boy who had impressed his teacher. "But you taught me. When you helped me, and we ran, you always made us stop to help others, even when I was so scared I couldn't breathe. You taught me. We have to help the ones he hurts. But we've always helped after he hurt them. Let's help stop him before he hurts more. Wouldn't that be easier?"

Ella smiled, and for a moment, the scar that bothered her so seemed to fade away and Rafe saw the lovely woman she should have been. The clear, direct blue gaze swung to meet his and she shook her head. "We aren't leaving, Rafe. This may be your land—I knew the moment you came here, I felt it. I knew a Master was here, a new one. And you are worthy. But we aren't going to leave."

"You are scared to death of him," Rafe said through gritted teeth. "What can you hope to do? Damn it, you're barely stronger than a mortal. And..." his voice trailed off before he could finish. The words echoed in his head, though. *Robbie is little more than a child...*

Hypocrite, he muttered to himself. He had railed at Ella because she didn't want Robbie feeding a vampire. And now Robbie wanted to help fight a vampire, but Rafe was acting as though he wasn't good enough.

Scrubbing his hands across his face, he swung around and saw Dominic standing in the door, pale, but upright. There was a smirk on his young face, and Rafe bared his teeth at him. "What in the hell are you snickering at?" he demanded.

Dominic lifted one shoulder in a careless shrug. "You told me to get strong and get some of my own back. How in the hell can I do that if I leave?"

"Bloody hell!" Rafe roared, glaring at them all. "Did you all have nothing better to do but listen to a *private* conversation?"

Ella had the grace to look away. Robbie simply stared at them, smiling that fey smile that looked so out of place on a grown man's face. But Dominic lifted his chin pugnaciously and snapped, "Well, not really. It *is* daylight and I've developed this phobia of the sun. And in case you haven't noticed, we're in a damned tight space. Kind of hard to *not* hear, since the walls seem thinner than paper. And you don't exactly speak quietly, hotshot."

Rafe lifted his lip at him in a snarl, but Dominic just stood there, not even blinking.

Turning, he met Sheila's gaze and he had to fight the urge to turn her over his knee and spank that delectable ass. Or shake her. *Anything* to make her listen. "This is your fault," he muttered.

She smiled serenely.

With a sigh, Rafe crossed to her and placed his index finger under her chin, lifting her face to his. Lowering his head, he purred in her ear, "If you get hurt, so help me God, you'll be sorry."

Then he covered her smiling mouth with his for a gentle kiss.

Turning around, he surveyed his small army.

Damn it, what in the hell had he gotten into?

* * * * *

Robbie held the connection as Rafe spoke with Lori. The big witch with the slow, quiet voice and childlike ways had surprised him once more. As he had paced across the room, he had muttered, "Damn it, wish I could get in touch with Lori."

Telephones didn't always work very well for the witch. That normally wasn't an issue—for *her*. But when somebody who wasn't a witch needed to talk with her, it sucked.

Robbie had just smiled that slow vacant smile as he had reached out and touched his fingers to the silvery surface of the platter on the table before him. When he had pushed it toward Rafe, the surface had gleamed with a silvery light.

So now Rafe spoke with Lori, watching as the slim redhead stood there brooding, her mouth pursed, brows low over her pretty eyes. "They told you his name was Pierre?" Lori asked.

"For the second time, kitten," he said patiently. "*Yes.* They called him Pierre."

She scowled and shoved a hand through her hair, her fingers tangling in the red-gold curls. "There was a vampire who was in Louisiana. He was the one who bit Leandra. But he was more than a vampire. He was a witch."

"I heard about the vampire who changed Leandra," Rafe said quietly, lifting his brows. "But witch and vampire—that's not possible. The two powers don't combine. It's like when a witch and a shifter have a child. The powers cancel each other out."

"Did you forget about Leandra?" Sheila asked quietly from behind. "She is both vampire and witch—remember? And Benjamin Cross is both, shifter and witch."

Even as she mentioned them, Rafe thought of them. Leandra, Cross—both of them were the good guys. But what if one of their kind ended up on the wrong side...

"Can he be killed?"

Rafe slid Sheila a glance as she stepped to his side, staring into the surface as she met Lori's eyes. "Hey, Sheila," Lori said, her lips quirking in a slight smile. "I see the brooder found you."

"Yeah, girl, he found me," Sheila murmured, and Rafe felt her fingers entwine with his. "About Pierre, can he be killed?"

Lori laughed. "There is no creature, mortal or otherwise, on this earth that can't be killed. No matter what all the shows on TV tell you. There is no evil that can't be killed. Just like there's no warrior on our side who is infallible. Even Malachi can be killed. He's just a little harder to catch." One lid dropped in a quick wink and she added, "Thank God."

Rafe had to echo that sentiment, even as he wished that Lori wasn't feeling so talkative. "So he can be killed?"

Lori grinned. "Of course he can. Sunlight probably won't do it—I suspect he's old. So unless you can hold him down for several hours until the sun cooks him well-done, it won't do you any good to try that route. But beheading will do it, I imagine. Taking his heart. A stake would do it, but you have to remember, the older a vampire, the denser their bones become. His could be as solid as granite by now."

"Meaning getting through his chest to stake his heart won't be that easy?" Rafe drawled, rolling his eyes. "And I was thinking of trying to pull the bad-ass slayer act and stake him."

Lori cocked a brow at him and chuckled. "Here I was thinking you'd use that sword you like to carry around."

Sheila giggled. "He's going to use his cock?"

Lori burst out into laughter. "Well, that wasn't the one I was talking about. And actually, with this one, that would just make Pierre want to add Rafe to his stable. Rafe's such a pretty man…and Pierre likes it both ways," Lori said, waggling her brows at Rafe.

Rafe felt something sick crawl through his belly, but he had already known that. Vividly, he had known. The memories that tormented Dominic had shown him far too much. "You've become an evil brat, Lori, you know that?"

That same impish grin lit her face for a minute before it faded away. The sparkle in her eyes died and she gazed at him somberly. "Rafe, you need help. Pierre is an evil, powerful bastard."

A dry laugh escaped him as he gazed at Robbie over the table. "I've got help."

Lori simply stared at him, arching a brow, doubt gleaming in her eyes.

Rafe sighed, reaching up and pressing his hands to his face. The thought of another vampire coming in here, whether he was there to help or not, simply enraged him, even the thought of it. His hold on this land was too tenuous. Not even concrete yet.

Lori's brows drew low over her eyes as she stared at him. "What's going on, Rafe? You've never been too stupid to let anybody help you before. What's the deal?"

"It's the land, Lori."

Rafe cut his eyes to Sheila as she gently nudged him out of the way. "The land?"

Rafe moved away from the mirror, blocking their voices out. He couldn't do this. He couldn't keep people from coming if it would help but the thought of *letting* people into his land made him want to gnash his teeth and howl like a wolf. The fury the thoughts brought him was almost as intense as the rage he'd felt when he'd seen Dominic crouched over Sheila's nude body, plunging his dick inside the snug well of her pussy.

He closed his eyes as the fury arced through him, driving his hands through his hair, locking his fingers behind his neck. Crouching in front of the fire, he stared into the dancing flames, blanking his mind in an attempt to let the fury drain out of him.

* * * * *

Sheila kept one eye on Rafe as she spoke to Lori through the connection Robbie still held flawlessly.

"What do you mean it's the land?"

"I mean just that," Sheila murmured, keeping her voice low. "He bonded to it. I think the minute he hit Tennessee, he started to feel it. He tracked me from more than a hundred miles outside of Memphis—knew I was here. It was the land. The land knew him and started whispering to him the moment he got here."

"Bonded. As in Rafe has found his own territory?" Lori asked quietly. Her eyes slid to a point beyond Sheila and she suspected the witch was studying Rafe. Lori sighed, looking down for a moment and the red-gold of her curls spilled into her face. "I think Eli knew this was coming. He's been so tense lately. And you leaving... Sheila, I thought he was going to go insane for a little bit there. He attacked Eli."

Sheila's jaw dropped. Turning, she stared at Rafe, but he didn't seem to have heard as he stared into the fire, his face stark, eyes burning. *Attacked* Eli? Damn it, Rafe was more than two hundred years younger than Eli. Rafe was strong, fast, and would be one hell of a Master. If he lived long enough. Attacking vampires centuries older than him wasn't going to increase his life span.

Lori chuckled. "I think he surprised Eli." Then her face sobered and Lori sighed. "He's young. Except for

Byron, he will be the youngest to ever claim his own territory. At least here."

"He can handle it," Sheila said with a slight smile. She had no doubt of that.

"And you'll be going with him?"

Sheila arched a golden brow at Lori in response. Lori just laughed. Her head cocked to the side, as though she heard something in the distance. But the clouding of her eyes made Sheila think it was something else. Then her face went smooth, blank as a doll's, lids drooping low until barely a sliver of green showed.

Sheila stayed quiet, waiting. When Lori's eyes opened, they were glowing. "I'll talk with Leandra. If Pierre is in Memphis, she's a good woman to have at your side."

"If Malachi comes here..."

A Master as powerful as Malachi would edge a new Master like Rafe into fury, Sheila knew. Shaking her head, she cut herself off and said, "No. Malachi can't come here right now. He can't."

Lori laughed. "I wasn't planning on talking to Mal, sweets. I'm going to talk to Leandra. And I imagine she can slip away from Mal. She's done it several times already. Mal doesn't keep her on a leash."

Chapter Six

Leandra scowled at Lori's image in the mirror, poking out her lip petulantly. "What makes ya tink I care where dat bastard is?" she said sullenly, even though fury was burning hot and bright in her belly. Of course, she cared. She hadn't seen a sunrise in months. Tried to watch the sunset, against Mal's advice, and got third-degree burns for her trouble. She hadn't eaten a damned hot fudge sundae or had a milkshake since that bastard had bitten her, forcing Mal's hand. Malachi had changed her, reluctantly.

Leandra didn't blame him—in fact, she was grateful to the arrogant bastard, not that she'd let him know.

But she *hated* that bastard who had forced this on her. Hated him with a passion. Wanted him dead. Eviscerated. Castrated. Then beheaded. So he died slowly.

Lori laughed and Leandra blinked, not aware that her fangs had slid down. "That look on your face makes me think you care, Leandra. You want him or not?"

Leandra simply stared at Lori for a long moment, but the witch just smiled sunnily at her. "Of course you want him," Lori concluded. "There's one slight problem though."

Rolling her eyes skyward, Leandra shook her head. "And what problem would dat be, Lori?"

"You can't let Mal come."

Leandra's jaw dropped and she simply stared through the mirror's surface. After a minute or two, she finally just grinned and shook her head. "Lori, my friend, and how am I supposed to tell him dat? He's training me."

"Just don't tell him."

Leandra narrowed her eyes. "Malachi is de one who brought me over, Lori. I don't have to *tell* him anything. He knows." Rolling her eyes, she leaned toward the mirror and winked. "And I do mean he knows...everything."

Lori closed her eyes and murmured, "I suspect Malachi was being a bad boy?"

"A Peeping Tom." Then Leandra pursed her lips into a thoughtful frown. "Well, it was more like—telepathic voyeurism, I tink. Since he didn't ever show up."

Lori tried to stop the snicker. Leandra had to give her credit for that. But her lips kept twitching and her mouth curved up and before she could stop it, the witch was laughing, tipping her head back and giggling. The giggles turned into guffaws as Leandra scowled at her and then tears started to roll down her face.

"Oh, that is rich," Lori managed to gasp out. "You are so—well, you are Leandra."

Leandra scowled, her brows drooping low over her eyes. "I am. And why does that amuse you so much?"

Lori's mouth was still curved in a smug smile. "Because you might well be the female equivalent of Malachi. Given a few hundred years," Lori snickered. "Enigmatic, intimidating...well, you don't intimidate me, but then again, neither does Malachi. But damn near everybody else, you so much as look at them and they turn white with fear. Malachi does that to people. Nobody could better suit you. So, have you done it yet?"

Leandra's face screwed up. "No! With...with *Mal*?"

Lori's mouth curved in a grin. "Of course. With Mal. I can't breathe when it comes to Jonathan, but, well...I'm not dead. And Mal could make an angel want him...We aren't angels, Le."

Leandra shook her head, humor dancing in her eyes. "I don't want him." She shrugged, one smooth caramel-colored shoulder lifting up as she shifted her gaze, staring into the distance. "Mal is, well, he is Mal. The closest ting to a father, or a brother, that I have. And I don't want him."

Lori's brows lifted as Leandra sighed, shaking her head. "Wanting...it's worthless. When it lasts longer than a few minutes, it brings nothing but heartbreak."

When Lori asked, "And who is it you want?" Leandra turned away from the mirror, and from Lori's knowing eyes.

* * * * *

Mike stood outside Lori's door, hearing her low murmur. The exotic voice he heard speaking back to her had an odd echo. They were speaking using magick, a mirror, window, anything that cast a reflection.

Even though the voice wasn't terribly clear, Mike knew exactly who it was.

His gut didn't burn with anger, even though he still had the scar from when she had shot him.

He did burn, though. Just hearing that voice, distorted as it was, made him hard. Made him hungry. Made him want...damn it, he'd been wanting her for so damned long.

Even when he lay bleeding on the floor of the car, he had wanted her. Had hated himself, because she was the reason a friend was dead.

Five seconds of staring into her tormented eyes hadn't alleviated the self-hate.

Seeing her eyes had.

She'd hated who she was.

Her father had tried to sell her into prostitution and she had run. The child she had been hadn't clearly seen the people who had taken her in. Leandra had been brainwashed. Plain and simple.

Only now did she look back at her life with clarity, and what she saw made her sick inside.

Mike had seen it in her eyes, the one time they had met since she had shot him.

Turning away, he moved silently to his room. Why did she haunt him so? Not like he'd ever seen any sign that she had similar thoughts about him. Oh, he was sure she regretted his blood on her already stained soul.

But he imagined she never lay awake at night, or day, thinking of him. Wondering about him. Shit, she was with *Malachi*.

The vampire was enough to make the hairs on his nape raise, his power was so strong. And women—they had a hard time resisting the call of a vampire. Whether they truly wanted him or not.

As ancient as Malachi was, the bastard left a flock of swooning, sighing women behind him everywhere he went.

Fury rippled through Mike at the thought of that. The skin on his spine went tight and for one long moment, he felt his temperature soar as the fury spiraled out of control.

Snapping a tight rein on it, he veered away from his room and jogged for the grand windows at the end of the hallway. He needed to run. Shoving them open, he leaped from the balcony, twenty feet high, and when he hit the ground, it was in the form of a giant timberwolf.

* * * * *

As Lori broke the connection with Leandra, she felt the ripple of power that rolled through the air as somewhere near, a shape-shifter changed. The fury that blistered the air during the change made her shiver.

It wasn't Jonathan.

She could feel him, like an echo of her own heartbeat.

The long eerie howl rose, filling the night, and inexplicably, Lori felt her eyes fill with tears.

And she knew who it was.

There was only one wolf in the enclave that was that stricken with loneliness.

The door opened and Jonathan came through, his long, thick, brown hair hanging loose around his shoulders, chest bare. There was a mark, silvery, faintly bird-shaped, on his side.

And long, nasty scratches on his chest. They were slowly knitting together even as she stared at him, but they looked painful. "Well, honey," she said in a bright tone, giving him a vapid smile. "Looks like you had a rough day at the office."

Their eyes met and Lori felt something hot and sweet move through her.

* * * * *

Leandra was good at lying. She could do it without blinking a lash, without her heart skipping a beat, without any sign at all. There was no reason at all for her to be nervous as she sauntered into the living room of the house.

Malachi had moved them into the Smoky Mountains several months ago. She rather liked it. Especially with the ripe scent of fall in the air, the leaves changing colors...the sun setting earlier and earlier.

She could already take a little bit of sunlight. But she liked it when the night came earlier and lasted longer. Gave her time to get out of the house and *move*, do something. Something besides brood and train.

Of course, it was rather astounding that she had the energy to do anything. Malachi's lazy act was just that, an act. He was a brutal teacher, pushing her body to the very limits, teaching her things she never knew she could do, refining her instincts until she could hear a whisper from a hundred yards away.

Leandra had thought the refined senses of the vampires were purely instinct, natural. But they weren't. She had learned to understand those skills, refine them, before she could really put them to use.

But, damn...it was exhausting.

"Hello, Leandra."

She couldn't see Malachi, but that didn't mean he wasn't there. His voice was a low, soothing sound to her ears, but it echoed all around. Which meant he wasn't cloaking himself in the shadows, unless he'd learned how to throw his voice.

So he had shifted into an indefinable mist.

"Playing the voyeur again, are ya, Mal?" she drawled.

He laughed, and even though Leandra was one of the few who weren't drawn to him, that laugh stroked over her like a swath of velvet. Goose bumps broke over her body and she closed her eyes for a second, focusing, listening to the sound of her heartbeat, breathing in a slow, regular rhythm until the fog of lust cleared from her mind.

"Life is no fun, if ye don't play from time to time," Malachi said, and Leandra felt the power ripple down her spine as he shifted from mist into his mortal form.

"Then life should be plenty of fun for ya," she said dryly, rolling her eyes to the ceiling. "Seeing as how games are your favorite pastime."

"And it is probably rather dull for *you*," Malachi returned. "You don't play enough."

Perfect opening…Leandra had to fight to keep the smile from spreading across her face. Instead, she just crossed her arms over her chest and said, "Well, dat's what I want to talk to you about. I'm going to take a few days off. Ya been running me senseless for weeks and I'm tired. Not to mention how ya keep sending me back to Excelsior every other day."

"Laying it on a bit thick, aren't ye?" Malachi drawled, flopping onto the couch and staring at her with a smile dancing in his midnight blue eyes. "Ye had to go there four times, in three months. Bloody hell, Leandra, we could ha' made ye *stay* there. For four years, while you trained there. Isn't this a bit better?"

She spun away, hiding the smile on her face. Damn. She was good. "Mebbe. Ya can't know how aggravating it is, mon, having to answer to somebody for every little ting I do," she said, keeping her voice harsh, aggravated.

"Hmmm. Well, quite a while has passed since I was trained. But I do not imagine it is much pleasure being watched over all the time," Malachi said with a shrug. Closing his eyes, he said, "Go on with ye. Just be careful."

She held back the triumphant grin until she was out of the room.

Behind her, Malachi opened one eye, studying her retreating back.

She was up to something. What, he had no clue.

Running his tongue over his teeth he debated between following her and just letting her go.

He *could* find out...if he pushed. But her head was thick, and she had been a powerful thing even before she was bitten. With her, there was no way to probe without her knowledge.

And he didn't really feel he had the right to intrude on anybody's privacy — well, most of them. Leandra had certainly earned her privacy. Bloody hell, she reminded him so much of himself, eons and eons ago.

Closing his eye, he decided to just let her go. This was Leandra, for pity's sake. The girl knew how to take care of herself.

* * * * *

Rafe felt it the moment somebody new entered his land.

A vampire...his skin tightened and his fangs dropped as tension flooded his body.

It wasn't a Master. The mark of a Master, Rafe thought with a smile. He understood now what Eli had felt when he looked at him.

A Master could feel the potential of others, just as he was feeling now. Very powerful, but young. And female...there was a feline, female feel to the power that was unmistakable, something vaguely familiar.

But beyond that, he couldn't distinguish a thing, whether this person was a Hunter, or a feral, or even just a lone vampire who lived among mortals.

That ability would come with time, he'd heard, but for now...*nada*.

Some gut instinct whispered there was nothing to worry about—he was running on pure instinct at this point, so he accepted it, let it go.

If it was a threat, he suspected he would know.

Rafe heard the quiet footsteps behind him, smelled the sweet scent of Sheila's body as he stood staring into the fire, brooding.

"Still pissed we wouldn't leave?" she asked quietly.

Rafe glanced at her over his shoulder. "I don't know why I should be. I should have known you'd be stubborn about this."

Her lips curved up in a smile and she said sweetly, "I'm not being stubborn." He turned around and met her eyes, arching a brow. "I'm not. I'm being logical. I may not be the Hunter that you are, or that Sarel is...Jonathan, Eli, Lori—I could go on. But I *am* a Hunter. And I'm not weak. I can help. So can they."

Rafe ran a hand through his hair. "I don't doubt their heart. They hate him—I can see that easily. But, Belle, Robbie is barely able to read without help and he has to be reminded to take a bath, to eat. And Ella..." His voice trailed off as he thought of the diminutive little vampire. Oh, she wasn't the first child he had seen changed. Many didn't survive—the body of a young one just wasn't as capable of dealing with the change. But she wasn't the first.

Ella was the weak link though. She had the pallor of death, nearly gray, like a sick vampire and he suspected she barely fed enough to keep herself from starving or going insane.

And she was weak—so weak. There were humans, he suspected, who were stronger than she was.

Sheila gently said, "Baby, she's weak, yes. But she's smart. She remembers things, and she *knows* him. We need that. He's ancient. We can't beat him if we don't know what we are fighting."

He spun back around to stare into the fire, feeling its heat seep into his bones, basking in it. Quietly, he said, "He's a bad guy, Belle. That's all we need to know."

She moved up beside him and from the corner of her eye, he could see her studying him. "Not every bad guy is the same, Rafe," she said shortly. He watched as she drove a hand through her hair and glared at him in frustration. Her eyes narrowed and she whispered, "I'm right. You know I'm right."

He laughed. "Belle, just because I know you're right doesn't mean I have to like it."

Her lower lip poked out. "Damn it, it's no fun arguing with you when you know I'm right. I thought I was trying to convince you."

Rafe's lips curled up in a grin. "I can make it fun for you. Want me to pretend I'm not convinced?" he teased, reaching out and trailing a hand up her thigh.

She batted his hand away and he moved onto his hands and knees, crawling over in front of her, lowering his head to press a kiss to her knee. He heard her gasp and he skimmed his lips up farther, reaching for the hem of her skirt and pushing it higher.

Sheila's hands laced in his hair and she demanded, "What are you doing?"

He lifted his head slightly, grinning at her wickedly. "Trying to make this fun for you?" he offered whimsically.

Before she could respond though, Robbie came crashing through the door. His eyes were big and wild in his dark face, his hair tangled, flying around his face as he slowed to a stop, staring at them.

"What's wrong?"

Robbie's eyes jumped to Rafe's face, but then he looked away, crossing his arms over his chest and swaying from side to side.

Sheila rose, the hem of her skirt falling down around her ankles, a gentle smile on her face as she crossed over to Robbie. "What's wrong, sweetie?" she asked softly. Rafe watched as she reached up, rubbing Robbie's arm with the flat of her hand. Robbie stopped swaying, staring at Sheila with the desperation of a child frightened by a nightmare.

He swallowed. Tiny little lines fanned out from his eyes as he grimaced, fear written all over him. Harshly, he whispered, "There's somebody here."

"Here?" Rafe asked shortly, his eyes cutting around the room. He didn't feel anything...well, other than the new vampire who had made that blip on his internal radar.

"I can feel her—she's dangerous," Robbie whispered. "And angry—she's so mad."

Sheila muttered, "Damn it, this is the last thing we need." The butter-gold of her curls was disarrayed, tousled from her hands.

"Well, now. Dat's not the welcome I was expecting, mon—should I be leavin'?"

Robbie flinched and jerked away from Sheila, moving to the back of the room, cowering against the wall. Rafe didn't spare him a glance though. He knew that voice. For a brief second, he studied Sheila's face. There was relief there. And nerves.

She gave him a bright, false smile and then turned away, moving to crouch in front of Robbie. Rafe tuned out the soothing murmur of her voice as he turned and studied the woman standing in the door.

No wonder she had felt so familiar.

Leandra still looked the same. He hadn't seen her since the day she'd disappeared from Eli's enclave, but he knew nothing about her was the same. She was a vampire now, not just a witch. Born a witch, made a vampire after one had attacked her. Mal had changed her to save her life.

Of course, this was also the woman who had kidnapped Erika, and shot Mike. Mike wasn't the same man he'd once been—and this bitch was responsible. Her emotionless, amber-colored eyes stared coolly at him. She had eyes like a cat's. Reflecting the light back, blank and expressionless.

Leandra was a cool piece of work. He doubted anybody knew what was going on in that head of hers. Rafe didn't like that. A person who kept that much inside—he didn't trust them. Everybody showed emotion at some time.

"What brings you here, Leandra?" Rafe said levelly, even as he slid Sheila a look. He already knew. She'd spoken with Lori. He barely remembered bits and pieces from the past day—his mind was too full of all the stimuli he was absorbing from the land around him.

But she'd talked with Lori.

And Lori had sent Leandra.

She shrugged one smoothly rounded shoulder, a small smile dancing on the ruby-red of her lips. "Been hearing tings. A man I been lookin' for—I hear he's around," she drawled, sauntering in with a lazy swing of her hips, the thick black braids of her hair hanging down nearly to her butt.

"Been hearing, huh?" Rafe drawled.

Sheila smiled angelically at him. "Just because I didn't see the sense in leaving doesn't mean I didn't see the sense in your words. We needed help. She's help. And she's got a serious grudge against him."

Looking away from Sheila, he looked back to Leandra.

"This is your land," the witch said quietly, her lashes drooping until just a thin sliver of golden-amber showed. She took a deep breath, and her slim body seemed to shudder for the briefest of seconds. "I felt it, the moment I entered. The land is relieved. Much evil has been done here…"

Her eyes closed completely, and Rafe watched as the air around her seemed to shimmer. When her eyes opened, they glowed. A wind drifted through the room and the thick rows of her braids blew back from her face. Her gaze cut to the left and Rafe turned to see Ella cowering in the corner, staring at Leandra with terror.

"Leandra, she is not a threat," Rafe said in a low voice.

Leandra's eyes were vague, staring at nothing as a fey, mysterious smile curved her lips. Although she gazed toward Ella, Rafe had a feeling she didn't see the vampire…or at least, she didn't see Ella as she was now.

The feel of magick danced on the air, tightening, until an unreal tension all but flooded the air.

And then it was gone. Leandra's eyes focused as she stared at Ella, the amber of her gaze glowing as she whispered, "I know…she's salvation."

And the glow faded as she reached up, touching two fingers, the nails slicked with the same seductive red as her lips, to her brow. "That was…intense."

Rafe heard the increased pace of her heart and he wondered at it. She wasn't afraid. But she was something. What, he didn't know…nervous, perhaps. Anxious. Worried.

Something. But, like many things about Leandra, this was unclear, nebulous.

"You're pretty."

Rafe turned to see Robbie standing there staring at Leandra with that wide, innocent smile on his ageless face. Turning back to Leandra, he said, "This is Robbie. He and Ella have been here for a while."

Leandra's mouth curved in a smile unlike any Rafe had ever seen from her before. "Hello, Robbie. You're not so bad yourself."

Rafe stood by cautiously, watching as Leandra moved closer to Robbie. Sheila's hand closed over his and she leaned into him, whispering almost soundlessly against his ear. "Stop worrying so much. She's a good person, Rafe."

He couldn't quite believe that. But Robbie was staring at her with total trust as she moved closer. The terror from minutes ago was gone.

"Been here a while, eh?" Leandra murmured. "You ran a long time, didn't ya?"

Robbie nodded quietly. When her fingers came up to press against his temples, he just stood there.

Rafe stared at her, feeling the magick shudder through the air.

"She's a witch?"

Ella spoke in a low, confused voice just behind him. Turning his head, he saw her fear. Forcing a reassuring smile, he said, "A powerful one. One of the most powerful ones we've ever seen."

Ella licked her lips, and the scar bisecting her face twisted as she scowled, staring at Leandra with confusion. "But she's a vampire. I feel it. She'll be a Master one day."

"I was born a witch," Leandra said. Still standing by Robbie, she continued in a bored tone, "But then dat bastard who made ya got a hold of me. Tried to kill me, and would have. But I got me some good friends. One of them saved me."

She sure as hell was a mistress of understatement, Rafe mused. It was a lot more complicated than, but she'd summed it all up in just a handful of words.

"What are you doing to Robbie?" Ella demanded. Her voice trembled and shook, and fear all but oozed from her.

But she was such a brave little thing, Rafe thought. His heart broke as he thought of her.

Leandra didn't so much as glance their way, but her voice was gentle as she responded, "Talking to your friend here, baby. He has so much buried inside his mind, but he can't understand it, much less tell us."

"Don't hurt him!" Ella whispered harshly.

Rafe turned to her, kneeling in front of her. "Ella, look at Robbie. He doesn't understand a lot of things, but he knows human nature. She won't hurt him—he knows that. Trust him, even if you can't trust her."

* * * * *

Leandra felt lost in the pure gold of the man's soul.

She could see back, so far back. He must be three or four hundred years old. His memories were muddled... everything seemed to be little more than image and color to her, like the way she'd expect a child's thought processes to be. No words. No goals in mind. Nothing beyond Ella and safe.

Safe.

That was how he thought of it.

And safe was away from the bad guy.

The man's face was distorted, but she'd recognize those eyes anywhere. As he thought of the bad man, the images that moved through Robbie's mind were harsh and over-bright. Like looking at a reflection from a carnival mirror, she supposed.

Heavy black clouds of fear rose up, obscuring his thoughts and his memories from her. Fists would come flying out of the darkness and the pain was obscene, even in memory.

And then...Ella.

He saw her standing in the shadows, dressed like a little doll.

The scars that Leandra had glimpsed on the petite vamp's face were smoothed out. He saw her as whole and perfect, and he adored her. She was his safety, his heaven, his world…everything.

It wasn't a love that was sexual at all. It was pure.

She was all to him.

Leandra's heart ached as she pulled her hands away. Her mind was buzzing with the information she had gathered from him, but it was bitter.

Turning away, she stared at Ella and felt the same thing deep inside of her.

Swallowing, Leandra stalked past them, grabbing her bag and shoved the door open.

It hurt…that much love.

The thought of love shouldn't bring pain.

Unless it was a person who would never know love.

* * * * *

Sheila followed Leandra out the door.

For one moment, she'd seen pain in the woman's exotic eyes.

Pain so dark and deep, Sheila ached just looking at her.

Closing her eyes, she stood there and breathed in the air. She couldn't hear Leandra, but the subtle perfume of the lotion she wore was still in the air. She found the witch perched on the hill just outside the caves where Ella and Robbie had set up their little home.

Casting a look over her shoulder, she said brightly, "They picked a nice spot to stay at while they are here."

"This isn't a spot — it's home to them." Sheila watched as Leandra slid her a narrow look and added, "Dey been here more den thirty years, girl. Long time, dey been running."

Sheila blinked, her steps slowing to a stop. "Thirty years?"

Leandra's mouth quirked in a small smile. "Been more than a century since dey got away." Her face sobered and she shook her head. "How did dey get away...I couldn't see it in his mind. Clouded. His mind is so clouded."

"They were hurt," Sheila said quietly. "I don't know how badly..."

Leandra's voice was brittle. "I got me an idea of how bad. Very bad. Bad enough that his mind shut off the memories just to protect him." She laughed and Sheila winced at the high, jagged sound. "Protect him. Poor bastard — where in da hell were the Hunters when dis was being done to him?"

Sheila sighed as she moved to Leandra. Lowering herself to the ground, she smoothed out the long, flowing skirt she'd pulled on earlier. She couldn't resist comparing herself to Leandra, the exotic dark beauty with her ruby red lipstick, her hair woven into numerous skinny braids, and that tough as nails attitude, her long, sleek curves poured into form-fitting black.

Total opposites...it sometimes confounded Sheila that she could relate so well to Leandra.

Leandra was a warrior, bred to the bone.

Sheila had been born wanting little more than to nurture.

But they had both ended up in the same place.

Forcing her mind back to Leandra's question, Sheila said quietly, "I wish I had an answer to that. They saved themselves—I don't know how. Ella won't tell us, although I suspect she remembers. Robbie, well, he can't. You saw that. They saved themselves, and I don't want to think about what it cost them. We should have been there, and for some reason, we weren't."

Leandra's full mouth flattened out into a firm line— her eyes glittering, glowing in the dim light. "I know why." She held out one hand and Sheila watched as a golden orb, shot through with light and mist, formed, swirling in a circle too fast for the eye to track.

The mists coalesced into a form within the glowing ball. A face appeared...a rather lovely looking man, entirely too pretty. Except for those soulless eyes. A great, empty maw—and even though he wasn't standing there before her, she felt as though she was staring straight into hell.

A shiver raced down Sheila's spine as Leandra said flatly, "He's the why."

"Pierre?"

Leandra barely even acknowledged her as she reached up, trailing one ruby-red fingertip over a faint scar on her neck. "He just wanted to feed on me...so he could get away from Mal. He's afraid of Malachi, very afraid, dat one. Wanted de strength that feeding on a witch could give him. He'd been injured. Killing me would have just been the means to an end." Her eyes closed, her head lowered, as she whispered, "Didn't care. He didn't care at all that I would die, so long as he got what he wanted. And dat...it is probably de least of all his evils."

Her voice trailed off for a minute, and when she spoke, it was in a flat, emotionless tone. "Wherever he goes...he creates a null around him. Like he's not dere...and dere's fear in de air. People shy away from it...Hunters shy away from it...without even knowing why. And dat is why we weren't dere."

Even though her voice was flat, Sheila sensed a deep pain inside the other woman. Instinctively, she reached up, wrapping her arm around Leandra's shoulders, hugging the younger woman to her.

One of her hands came up and closed over Sheila's hand, squeezing it. "I have seen some great evil, Sheila. Ya know dat? Done more evil than I can easily live with. Most of it blindly. But it pales. Compared to him."

Sheila felt something dark and cold move through her at Leandra's words. "What in the hell are we getting into?" she murmured, shaking her head. Shoving a hand through her hair, she caught the locks in a loose tail at the nape of her neck, staring out at the twinkling lights of the city.

Leandra chuckled. A low, warm sound as she flopped back against the ground, staring up at the sky. Sheila fell back with her, studying the witch from the corner of her eye. "A vampire, Sheila. He just be another vampire...little stronger, little harder to kill...but he can be killed."

Sheila grimaced. "Any bright ideas on how to do it?"

Leandra grinned slyly and said, "I tink a barbeque would be nice."

* * * * *

"Where is he?"

Leandra just shook her head as she let go of Robbie's hand. "He can't tell me. Nothing I can go by, at least."

Rafe turned to stare at Ella, arching a brow. "Where is he, Ella?"

Ella shook her head, wrapping her arms around her body. "I don't know. We ran here, didn't think he would follow. I don't even know if he realizes we are here. We've been here so long..." She smiled shakily and shrugged, tears rolling down her face. "We aren't worthy of his notice, Rafe."

He moved over to the chair she huddled in and knelt in front of her, smiling gently. Anytime he spoke with her, he felt like he was talking with Erika. Even though Ella was centuries old, there was something childlike about her, something that went deeper than just her body, fifteen forever.

"How did you know he was here?" Rafe asked softly, catching her chin when she tried to avert her face.

The scar that bisected her face puckered around her mouth as she dragged her tongue across her lips. Raising one shoulder in a shrug, she said, "I felt him. He has a taint that you cannot mistake."

Rafe blew out a breath and patted her knee before he stood. Turning, he studied Leandra with an arched brow. "Well?"

Leandra returned the look and said, "What?" Then she turned away, shaking her head and muttered, "Always wanting someting. Ya tink I know someting? Why in dey hell would ya tink I know someting?"

Shrugging, he said, "Well, do you?" When she just curled her lip at him, he laughed. "That's what I thought. What do we do?"

Leandra crossed her arms over her chest, and replied, "We do not do a ting. I have to do it. Mebbe I should jus' get me ass back to Malachi. What in de hell am I doing…"

Rafe smiled as she walked away muttering, shaking her head and raking her hands over her head, fisting the thick braids in her hands.

'Well, she looks happy to be a part of the team," Sheila said brightly.

"She scares me," Ella whispered.

Rafe grinned. "She scares a lot of people, but I don't think we need to worry about her."

Ella shook her head, not looking convinced. "That woman is dangerous — it colors the very air around her."

Rafe nodded, listening as the door slammed shut. He knew when she left the house. Like he was holding a fistful of marbles, and one had fallen out, he felt a shifting inside his being caused by her leaving. Damn — Eli had eight different vampires within his enclave, and three who lived solitarily in town. Was he always this aware of his people?

Looking back to Ella, he said, "Leandra is plenty dangerous. But she's on our side. It's the other side that needs to worry now."

With that, he turned and walked out.

Arching her brows, Ella stared at him, worried. "Now?"

Sheila chuckled at the deer-in-the-headlights look on Ella's face. The lady didn't miss a beat.

"Leandra has a complicated history," Sheila said quietly, patting the vampire's frail shoulder. "But don't worry. She's a white hat."

Ella's brows lowered and she frowned. "White hat?"

"Yes, a good guy." Ella wasn't hiding her face as much. Sheila found some pleasure in that, but her heart ached each and every time she looked at the delicate creature.

A lost cause. She couldn't help but come back to that thought whenever she thought of Ella. Couldn't see a happy ending for either Ella or Robbie. They were damaged, and they knew it. Sheila suspected something could be done for that hideous scar on Ella's face—Kelsey and Lori had worked wonders before, and the fact that the mark was centuries-old might not make that much difference to the powers the Healers commanded.

But nothing could be done about that fact that she had died when she was still a child.

Nothing could be done about Robbie, either, his mind forever that of a child's.

Sheila didn't know who she hurt for more, the man or the woman. Robbie knew something was wrong with him. He accepted it peacefully, but it still hurt him. Sheila could feel it every time he looked at Ella, his heart in his eyes.

Sheila felt something tighten in the air around them, and by the look in Ella's face, she had sensed it, too. Giving Ella a reassuring smile, Sheila said, "It's okay, baby. It's just Leandra."

"How can you tell? It's just magick…and magick can hurt," Ella whimpered, wrapping her arms around her thin body, swaying forward and back.

"Not all. Robbie's doesn't."

Ella gave Sheila a haunted look and said, "It can." I've seen him—he gets angry, and the magick turns bad.

Sheila arched a brow. "Has he ever hurt you?" she asked gently. "Or anybody who didn't deserve it?"

Ella shook her head even as she continued to stare at Sheila, petrified.

"Then it's not bad. It was protection, or justice. Ella, anything can be used to hurt people. The question is whether or not a person is using that power for their own end."

"And how can you tell if the magick is good or bad?"

Sheila lifted a shoulder. "I can just feel it—Leandra's magick feels a lot like Sarel's...a friend of mine. They are warriors, but they have hearts as pure as gold. Leandra has been misguided in her life, but she is a good person. Like your Robbie. He's got a warrior's soul."

* * * * *

Leandra felt him watching her.

Scratching another line into the muddy ground, she called out, "Wantin' to take a look, are ya? Come on and quit hiding in de shadows."

He moved soundlessly over the ground, but she sensed him coming up behind her and she shifted slightly to the right to let him have a better look.

"What are you doing?"

Something inside her wanted to weep as she looked up into his eyes. She hadn't ever seen a soul as pure as his. Or a heart as broken. He hid it well. She doubted anybody, even Ella, knew how sad he was. Robbie loved his Ella, the way a man loved his woman, yet he didn't even know how to handle it. He just knew that if Ella knew he was hurting, it would hurt her, so he hid it.

"Lookin' for him," she finally said, studying the box scratched into the ground before her. "Magick colors the air. I've made marks, for you, for me. A few other witches are around here, but not many. A little weird, I tink. Usually more witches around than this. But he scares people — they don't want t' be where he is."

"How can you find him, looking at dirt?"

She grinned. "I won't see dirt in a minute. Neither will you. Watch…" Lifting her hand, she spread it out, palm down, over the square. "Show me."

The box began to glow. Two bright lights gleamed at the bottom, near the center. "That's you and me, Robbie." The glow spread upward from their little bright specks and a few other specks appeared. Then the glow reached just a little up from the middle and the glow stopped.

A fierce, ugly splotch of color bloomed on the ground, a deep, violet-red with a border of green that pulsed as she stared at it. "And dat's him," she mused, cocking her head as she studied it.

He felt her searching for him. Leandra smiled coolly, while next to her, Robbie muttered soundlessly under his breath. Before Pierre could reach out though and try to track her, she swiped her hand across the ground, destroying the box, breaking the connection.

Her heart slammed against her ribs and she sucked in air, forcing her body to relax.

"He's bad," Robbie whispered, shaking his head.

"Yes, he is." Leandra reached up and squeezed his arm gently. "Don't worry, Robbie. He doesn't know where we are."

"Can't he do that, too?" Robbie asked, pointing at the ground.

She smiled slightly. "He could. But I know how to hide myself from prying eyes...and others. And I'm tinking dat his magick isn't as strong as he wants us to tink it is."

"His magick is strong." In a soft whisper, Robbie said, "He does hide—nobody's ever been able to find him."

"He's not as strong as he wants us to tink he is—he uses the magick of others to enhance his." Leandra shook her head. "And it's not that no one has ever been able to find him. He casts a spell of negligence—of thoughtlessness. They forget they even *should* look for him. People lose their purpose, without realizing it. But it's just illusion. Once ya know what to be prepared for..." her voice trailed off as she realized Robbie was staring at her in confusion. Forcing a smile, she just settled on, "Different kind of hiding, Robbie. He's hiding, but not the same way I am. I worried, a little, mebbe that he'd remember me if I searched dis way—but I don't tink he did."

She turned away, staring out into the night, focusing on the land under her feet, the sky overhead, drawing strength from them. The land hated the taint Pierre had wrought. It rejoiced in her presence, in Rafe's, although he probably wouldn't understand that.

Focusing on the serenity, she pulled it inside herself and tried to calm the fear that bubbled in her gut.

"He hurt you."

Turning on her heel, she met Robbie's eyes and nodded slightly. "That, he did. But in da end, that is what probably saved me."

She had a purpose now.

Amazing how that could make all the difference in the world.

Turning away, she never saw the appraising look on Robbie's face.

* * * * *

A purpose.

Late that night, past late, in truth, nearly dawn, he sat pondering the words he'd heard from the pretty witch. *I have a purpose now…*

She hadn't said them aloud. Just in her mind. But he'd heard them all the same.

Sitting on the floor by Ella's feet, he watched her carefully, making sure she took the blood he'd brought back for her. She didn't hunt. He had to feed her, but that was okay. She'd taken care of him for years when the bad man had taken him. She still took care of him.

A purpose…he wasn't sure he knew what that meant. He thought it meant having to do something. But he wasn't sure.

"Ella, what is a purpose?" he finally asked. She'd explain it to him. And she wouldn't make him feel like a dummy while she did it. A lot of people had made him feel stupid in his life.

And he knew he was. But Ella never made him feel that way.

"It's when there is something for you to do," Ella said as she daintily wiped the blood away from her lips with a napkin. "A goal, a place in life where you want to go. And you know you have to work to get there." Smiling down at him, she stroked a hand over his hair. "Like we knew we had to get away from *him*. That was a purpose."

Lowering his voice, he whispered, "What is a Hunter's purpose?"

Ella's eyes turned sad and Robbie wished he hadn't said anything. "A Hunter's purpose it to fight against the bad men, Robbie. People like him, who did this to us."

"Why does that make you sad?"

A tear fell down her cheek and Robbie wiped it away as she replied softly, "Because I'm not strong enough. And I want to be."

Robbie rested his head on her knee as he whispered, "You're strong, Ella."

"Not strong enough."

Propping his chin on her knee, he stared up at her and smiled, unaware of how that smile wrapped a fist around her heart. "You're strong," he repeated. "You saved me."

Ella laughed, leaning her head back as she set aside the mug that he had poured the blood into. "We saved each other, Robbie. We did."

No, Robbie thought, laying his head back down. She had saved him. All there was to it. He might have used the magick, but if she hadn't told him it would be okay, if she hadn't held his hand through the whole thing, if she hadn't given him a reason—a purpose—to even try to escape, he'd still be quivering in fear while Pierre fed off his strength.

Robbie was strong. But he knew he wasn't smart. He knew that...something that had been done to his mama while she had carried him had hurt his brain. But Ella cared about him anyway.

It was his turn.

His turn to save them all.

Pondering that, he smiled a little as he whispered, "A purpose…"

He had a purpose now.

* * * * *

Sheila rolled her eyes as Rafe bypassed her idea before she even finished speaking.

"Damn it, Rafe. *Think.* We need bait. Somebody a little stronger than the average human. But he knows Leandra, he knows Ella and Robbie. Dominic isn't strong enough yet and he's too new. And you—" she snorted. She skimmed her eyes over his long, lean form and said, "You practically shout Master Vampire. He likes his people a little easier than that."

"Then how do you explain Leandra?" Rafe drawled, arching a brow at her.

Leandra had that little smirk on her lips, but she met Sheila's eyes with an understanding smile. "Desperation, mon. He was desperate. He hunts de weak, Rafe. They surround him. Not physically weak, weak in de ways of power, weak up here." Tapping a red-tipped fingernail to her temple, she shrugged. "Sheila has a good plan, if ya would stop and tink it through."

"No."

Normally, when Rafe did that sexy growl thing with his voice, it made Sheila turn to lava inside. But for some reason, this time, she was just pissed off. Propping her hands on her hips, she sneered at him and said, "You got a better idea, slick?"

She watched, and smiled inside, as his eyes sparked with frustration. "No. But I will. One that doesn't put somebody in harm's way."

Sheila laughed. "Darlin', we're Hunters. Danger is what we do. I can understand wanting to keep Robbie and Ella safe, although they aren't unused to being around evil monsters. And they've got just as much right to see this ended as we do." Sauntering up to him, she smiled, laying one hand on his chest, covering his heart, while she used the other hand to cup around the back of his neck.

"Don't think you're going to put me in some china hutch where you can keep me safe and secure. Try it…and I'll go back to Eli. I haven't sworn myself into your service yet. And I won't—not until I know you're not going to turn into some obnoxious, overprotective ass."

His eyes glowed, gleaming with little flickers of red as he snarled down at her. "You're not going anywhere," he growled.

Sheila smiled sweetly at him, tucking a stray lock of hair behind her ear. "Try and stop me… According to the Council laws, you have no hold on me."

His hands closed over her arms—Sheila bit back a yelp as he jerked her onto her toes. "You are *mine*."

Okay, now that affected her. Sheila felt her legs turn to water and her belly started to heat. She could smell the musk of her own arousal on the air—her cheeks heated as she saw the answering hunger leap into his eyes while they stared at each other.

But fortunately, pride and feminine pique reared their heads and she jerked her head aside before he could slant his mouth over hers. "That may well be. But I will *not* be coddled. And if you try tucking me up on some shelf where I can sit all pretty and nice until you're ready to fuck me, I am *soooo* gone."

"You leave, I'll find you again," he growled.

"But you can't *make* me come back here," she growled back at him, the rage inside her finally catching up with the arousal. "I'll go to the council, damn it, and you know it."

The people around them seemed to fall away and Sheila forgot they weren't alone as Rafe whirled them around and pinned her against the wall. Her feet dangled in the air — against her chest, she could feel his heart. Hard, faster than it should beat, while twins flags of color appeared high on his cheekbones.

His voice was low and rough as he rasped, "You think they could keep you away from me? Death wouldn't stop me. Hell and all the demons in it can't keep me away from you."

Lifting her chin, she said coolly, "I can. If I don't want to be with you, then I won't be with you, Rafe. And I'll only be here if I get treated as something more than your pretty little fuck toy."

Shock, followed by anger, bloomed through his eyes. Her feet hit the floor as his fingers uncurled from her arms and he let go. "I don't think of you like that! Damn it, I just want to keep you safe."

Sheila whispered, "I want you safe, too. But if I tried to make you stay here all the time, hell, even once, you'd blow me off quicker than you can blink."

"It's not the same."

Sheila narrowed her eyes at him, and bared her teeth. "Why not? I'm a Hunter. You're a Hunter. I love you. You say you love me. Of course, you don't want me being who I am. You want a pet."

"I don't want a pet!" Rafe roared. The fury tore through him as he spun away and found himself staring into a pair of mild, amber-colored eyes. Leandra arched a brow at him, a cool smile on her lips. That smile...it was like somebody had turned a light on and he heard how he sounded to them. Turning back around, he stared into Sheila's icy eyes and said quietly, "I just want you."

"Then let me be me."

Rafe felt as though a fist had been closed around his throat as he looked into her eyes and saw the anger, the pain there. "Sheila... Belle, you don't understand. It kills me inside to think you being anywhere near him."

Sheila shrugged, her eyes dark, a bitter smile on her lips. "Do you think it's any easier on me when I see you leave? Hell, all I ever do is patrol. You get sent after the nasties out there—facing danger every time Eli sends you out on a job. Every night I worried you might not come back, that the sun would rise and you'd be gone, leaving me alone."

Shit.

He'd done the same, worried the same...even though her patrols were almost always quiet. And the nights that weren't—well, she may not be the strongest Hunter around, and she'd never be a Master, but she handled herself well.

Sheila was a careful fighter—one who picked her battles well. He couldn't say the same for himself. A fight came, and he plunged headlong into it. She planned, she paced herself...and she knew when she couldn't win, she knew when to walk away. Or run.

And if it was anybody but Sheila, he just might be willing to go along with the plan.

Which meant he was doing exactly what she had accused him of.

Overprotecting, coddling her. And that would drive her away as surely as his negligence of her months ago had led to her leaving

"I don't like it, Belle," he whispered, shaking his head.

Sheila arched a brow at him. "You think I do? But what else are we to do? He's here, Rafe, and he'll stay for as long as we allow it. This is *your* land. You have to protect it." As he watched, she shivered and her hands came up to rub at her arms. "The bastard's done enough damage here."

All the while, in the corner, Robbie stood watching.

Not one of them was aware of the thoughts circling through his mind.

Chapter Seven

Pierre saw the woman walking the streets.

A vampire...he hadn't realized another one had come into his lands. Oh, he'd felt the strong one, but this woman wasn't the one he'd sensed.

Odd—if another vampire had entered his lands, wouldn't he know?

Hmmm...she was quite delicious.

Long blonde curls, ripe curves under the long, glowing dress she wore. A young vampire—he loved the young ones. Especially the ones who walked all by themselves.

Of course, he was a little worried.

There were several new vampires in his hunting grounds.

That was never good. It too often meant Hunters were around.

Not this one though. She looked too soft. Too sweet.

Licking his lips, he watched her from the shadows as she moved up to the bar, smiling at the young man behind it.

Oh, yes. She was sweet.

Hungry, too, he imagined, from the way her eyes slid to the man's neck.

He'd let her feed.

After she fed, while she was still a little high, he'd move in on her then.

* * * * *

Sheila could feel him.

Dark, ugly, malicious…his essence permeated the air, and it was foul.

She could feel his eyes on her and she couldn't help but grin. Damn. He knew nothing of caution. At all.

But she wasn't ready to be taken. Not at all.

They had a plan…they knew what they needed to do.

She, on the other hand, needed to feed. But something told her this wasn't the safest place to do that. Sipping from the rum and coke she'd ordered, she tried to figure out the best way out of here without drawing too much notice to herself.

One that wouldn't involve Rafe roaring into town and drawing attention to himself.

There was no way this vampire Pierre was unaware of Rafe's presence, but being aware of his presence, and knowing *what* he was were two different thing. One look and Pierre would know a Hunter had come to town, and a Master at that.

Her mind worked furiously as she focused on Pierre, feeling him shifting around the room, still watching her.

A couple argued, a few feet away. Though they were screaming, through the din of the music and crowd, not many people had noticed them yet. Sheila heard, though. The guy had slid her a look when she came in, just like he'd been checking out every other female in the bar.

His date, apparently, was sick of it.

With a smile, Sheila leaned on the bar and focused a little on her own power. Her call was minor yet, but stronger since that night she'd taken blood from that man in the alley a few miles away. Just a week ago. It seemed so much longer...

It swelled within her, and rolled from her body like heat waves, unseen by everybody, but felt by all. Suddenly, many eyes were focused on her, including the man who was trying to defend himself against his girlfriend.

When he looked at her involuntarily, Sheila dropped her lid in a quick wink, making sure the girlfriend saw it.

When the girl threw herself at her boyfriend, chaos ensued.

With a pleased smile, Sheila faded into the shadows. She didn't disappear. She doubted she'd ever have the power to shift to mist, to wolf, to anything. But she could use shadows, and use them well.

And the coolest part was...it was almost innate, and required no magick, no focus, nothing. It could, for a little while, even obscure her presence from other vampires...providing they weren't her Master or her sire.

She slid out of the bar without Pierre even realizing she had left as people gathered around the tussling couple on the ground. By the time the woman was pulled off her date, still kicking and cussing, Sheila was gone.

* * * * *

Sheila sat in the corner, curled up on the cot where Dominic slept during the day, watching Rafe as he paced and brooded and growled under his breath. "Damn it, what in the hell were you thinking, going out alone?" he demanded. For the third time.

Repeating herself, she said, "I was thinking I was *hungry*. I haven't fed in two days, Rafe. I can't go days without feeding, babe."

Dominic sat by the fire, his arms looped around his knees. "I'm kind of hungry, too," he whispered, his eyes dropping to the ground as he spoke.

Sheila smiled angelically. "See? He's hungry, too, Daddy," she said cheekily. "The only person who fed last night was Ella. Well, Robbie…but he has a different diet."

Rafe's brows dropped low over his eyes, a threatening growl rumbling out of his chest as he glared at her.

Sheila threw her hair out of her eyes and rose from the bed. "Damn it, Rafe, stop growling at me," she snapped. "You keep it up and I'm going to think you're trying to turn me on. I am *hungry*. If I don't feed soon, I'm not going to be worth a damn thing. And if Dominic doesn't feed, then he's going to be in very bad shape. What do you want us to do, sit around and starve while you figure out what we are going to do?"

Leandra chortled in the background and Rafe's eyes cut to her. "What, you want to join in, witch?" he rasped.

Leandra smiled angelically. "I'm fine, thanks. Fed on me way in," she drawled. "I'm good for a day or so. I can tap into the land if I start feeling low."

Sheila muttered, "That's cheating."

Leandra just shrugged.

Rafe spun away and Sheila's gaze dropped down to study his butt, the way the jeans clung to that hard, muscled curve. Damn, what she wouldn't give to sink her teeth into that ass, feel the muscles of his back while she knelt astride him, rubbing her hands up and down the dips and planes of his back.

When he spoke abruptly, she jumped, pulling herself out of her little daydream, smiling sweetly at him.

"Fine, we'll go out. You, me, and Dominic. We'll feed tomorrow night. But we stay together. Pierre isn't the kind who's going to try to move on three at once."

"Won't he recognize me?" Dominic asked quietly.

Sheila said softly, "He might. But we'll have to risk it. You can't go without feeding for too much longer. And me…eh, I've gone a little longer than I like, too."

"He's out tonight. Chances are he'll use tomorrow to relax. Older vamps don't have to feed as much…"

His voice trailed off and he turned away.

"Does that mean he's out there now doing what he did to me?" Dominic whispered, rising from the ground.

"Not very likely," Rafe muttered. Sheila knew he didn't want to think about it much. "He won't need to feed that heavily for a good long while…and I think I'd feel it this time."

Sheila stilled. She hadn't thought of that. Eli was prone to sending people out randomly, to a new target, just out of the blue. Master vampires were entirely too attuned to their land and that was one of the reasons, so they could deal with the monsters that plagued their territory.

Dominic turned away, shaking his head. "This is too fucking much," he muttered, driving a hand through his hair.

"Too damned much."

* * * * *

"No way. That's too much—I can't just go and *bite* somebody."

Rafe suppressed the response that leaped to his lips as he dryly said, "What did you think we were going to do? Rob a blood bank? That's stealing."

"So is biting somebody to take their blood," Dominic muttered as they moved upstairs, following the sway of Sheila's hips.

"Yeah, well, people in a hospital aren't going to suffer if you take blood from a person... You steal it from a blood bank, you are depriving somebody who needs that blood. We don't steal...not when we can avoid it," Rafe replied. "And feeding from them isn't stealing...they want it. At least at the time."

He kept his eyes on Sheila's back, tuning Dominic's annoyed mutter out of his head. They had to feed. So far, he hadn't sensed anything from Pierre, not since last night. He'd felt that—known he was on the prowl. But it wasn't until Sheila came home with her little announcement that he realized she had been the prey.

"Nice outfit she's wearing," Dominic said abruptly.

Rafe felt the possessiveness stir as he glanced at Dominic and saw that the vampire was staring at Sheila's ass, outlined by a very snug-fitting pair of black leather pants. The top she wore left her back and arms bare, tied at the neck and at the waist, and she'd swept her hair up into a loose knot on top of her head. She wore a white gold collar-like necklace, and hammered white gold bracelets around her wrists.

She looked...hot.

Trolling clothes.

The club they'd hit was a rather…eclectic one. As a couple approached Sheila, Rafe figured out real quickly why she'd chosen this joint, and why she was baring so much flesh.

She'd brought them to a bondage club.

Well, he had said he wanted them to stay together, he told himself as she smiled flirtatiously at the woman, then darted a rather nervous glance at the man, before dropping her eyes coquettishly to stare at the floor.

She made a motion in his direction as the man bent his head to murmur in her ear, skimming a hand up Sheila's abdomen, his fingers trailing between her breasts to come up and toy with the necklace she wore.

Eyes slid in his direction, and Rafe cocked a brow, a smile lurking on his lips as he murmured to Dominic, "She is going to get her ass paddled for this."

"Well, if that's what she wants, she came to the right place." Dominic was staring down onto the lower level, watching one woman in particular as she walked through the club, a man crawling behind her with his head down, wearing nothing but a collar around his neck. "I wondered for a minute if she knew where she had brought us. Didn't think this was her thing."

Rafe smiled coolly as Sheila started to move in his direction. "It's not. Not generally. She had a reason for coming here, and she knows what kind of place this is."

Rafe and Dominic closed the distance between Sheila and the couple at her back. She smiled mischievously at Rafe before ducking her head, stepping aside and letting the man behind her move up to Rafe.

Rafe summed him up with one quick glance. New to this, and more in it for the thrill than anything. Probably talked his girlfriend into it, and he'd regret that. She got a thrill from it, all right.

And as soon as a real Dominant came along and caught her eye, this guy was history.

"You let your slave go trolling much?"

Rafe suppressed the urge to roll his eyes. *Let* Sheila? Damn it, he was lucky if he could just get her to use common sense. But he just smiled. "It's her birthday. Wanted to give her a nice present."

"Hmmmm."

Sheila stood admirably still as the man stroked a hand down her cheek, forcing her to look up at him. "She's very pretty — what did you have in mind?"

Fifteen minutes later, they had a room on the upper level of the club.

* * * * *

Sheila stood by, watching impassively as Rafe and Dominic held the woman between them. She looked like she was in heaven.

Jerks, she thought pithily. Her arms were tired. Stretched overhead, the cuffs looped over a hook in the wall, Sheila had been watching them make out for damn near ten minutes. While *she* had to tolerate the man next to her sliding his hands over her every few minutes, bending to murmur in her ear, "I like to watch a woman eat pussy. Maybe after they are done with her, that's what we'll do."

Wannabe. Sheila kept her eyes down though, making the appropriate noises under her breath.

Their names were Jake and Beth — and Sheila's plan had worked to a "T". Rafe wanted them to stay together, and other than Hunting, this was the best way to ensure it, and there was privacy.

Of course, she hadn't exactly expected it to make her so damned hot...watching Rafe run his hands over the woman while he kept lifting his head to stare at her.

He lifted his head again, and this time, she smiled back. His fangs had dropped. Beth was moaning feverishly as Dominic pumped his fingers in and out of her pussy.

"Now," Rafe murmured in a low tone.

Sheila lifted her eyes at that moment and jerked down with her hands. The hook came out of the wall with a crack and the man turned, looking startled. Sheila focused, and the air in the room tightened around her as the vampire's call rolled from her.

A dazed look entered Jake's eyes and she reached for him, rising on her toes to cup his head, arching his neck. She struck, and the blood flowed into her—hot, ripe. His cock pumped against her belly, and Sheila shuddered as lust billowed through her.

Watching Rafe and Dominic with Beth had made her hot.

Entirely too hot.

When Jake's hands closed over her ass, she whimpered and rubbed herself against him. The seam of her leather pants slid wetly over her flesh—the scent of her arousal drifted through the air, mingling with the scent of sweat, male hunger, and blood.

"She looks like she's having entirely too much fun."

Rafe's hands closed over her shoulders and she groaned as he cuddled his cock against her ass. His lips cruised over her neck, up to her ear where he purred, "Enough, Sheila."

Lifting her head, she licked her lips. Glancing at Rafe over her shoulder, she said, "I know when to quit."

"Good to know."

Scowling, she glanced at Dominic as he eased Jake's body from her and slid him to the ground. "You going to put the whammy on him?"

Arching a brow at him, Sheila drawled, "The whammy?"

Dominic smiled. "Yeah. Whatever you always did to me to make sure I was sleeping until long after you'd gone."

Sheila shrugged. "No reason. He's not going to wake up for a few minutes, and we're leaving."

"No."

She narrowed her eyes at Dominic, then shivered as Rafe stroked his hands down her arms.

Dominic was smiling. A real smile, something she hadn't seen in a while. But it was hot, hungry, and entirely too predatory, not that laid-back smile she was so used to.

"No," Rafe echoed, lowering his head to rake his teeth over her neck. "We're not."

Arching a brow, Sheila drawled, "The bondage thing isn't really my scene, boys."

Rafe slid a hand down the middle of her body, palm flat, fingers widespread. As he cupped his hand over her mound, she bit her lip. Heat spiraled through her, teasing senses already heightened by watching Rafe and Dominic with Beth.

"Hmmm, maybe not, but you're hot," he whispered against her cheek, the stubble from the late-day shadow abrading her skin. "Very hot...and very wet, I bet. You liked watching us with her, didn't you?"

Dragging her eyes from Dominic's face, she arched her head away. "You got some nice moves on you, Rafe. Dominic, too. It's not a hardship to watch you use them."

Rafe smiled a little. "Maybe we should wake her up then...practice those moves a little." She felt the cool metal of the cuffs and started to pull away, but Dominic chose that moment to move up, crowding her against Rafe. Caught off-guard, she was cuffed before she even had a chance to blink. "And you can stay here and watch."

Sheila's lip curled. "Bite me," she said pithily. Watching Rafe touch Beth made her hot, but there was no way in hell she was going to watch him fuck her.

"Don't worry." The low whisper made her body tighten with anticipation. "I will...but maybe you should put him under first."

As Rafe spoke, they all heard a low moan, and as one, the three vampires turned their gaze to Jake who lay on the floor, eyes fluttering a little.

"Sleep," Sheila whispered, reaching out with her mind to touch his. He slid into sleep then, a deeper sleep that would last for hours.

Looking back, she flicked her gaze from Dominic to study Rafe over her shoulder. Tugging with her hands, she tested the cuffs. Reinforced — Rafe's, most likely. She hadn't brought any, since she hadn't planned on doing any Hunting.

They were waiting for her. Waiting to see her reaction, or maybe to give her a chance to put a halt to it. Curling her lips into a slow smile, she tossed her hair over her shoulder and said, "What are you waiting for...an invitation?"

Her gasp of excitement was muffled against Dominic's mouth as he kissed her. Behind her, she felt Rafe's hands, moving gently, a pointed contrast to Dominic's greedy mouth. His fingers stroked up the naked skin of her back, tugging at the ties that held her shirt in place at the waist and neck.

Cooler air stroked over her torso as the shirt fell away. Her nipples tightened, aching. One of Dominic's hands cupped a breast, his thumb and forefinger plucking one plump, puckered nipple as his tongue slid demandingly into her mouth.

She sucked on it greedily, biting down gently and smiling inside as she felt his response in the way his body tightened, how the sound of his heartbeat stuttered right before it sped up.

Rafe's hands moved over her hips and she quivered as he slowly tugged the zipper down, his hands stroking down her hips, taking the snug-fitting leather as he moved.

His mouth pressed against her ass, kissing first one cheek, then the other as he tugged away her boots. Seconds later, she was completely naked. Rafe stood up, moved in, pressed against her, so that she was sandwiched between the two men.

Dominic fell to his knees in front of her, taking one nipple in his mouth, tormenting the other with his fingers. "Damn it, I love your tits," he muttered against her. "You're so fucking perfect."

Rafe's hand cupped her cheek, forcing her to look at him. Craning his head around, he covered her lips with his, swallowing the soft moans falling from her lips. Her head felt too full — too full of emotion, too full of sensation, too full of *Rafe*. His voice seemed to whisper inside her head as he kissed her. *Perfect, and mine. All mine...he can touch your body, if I let him, but he won't ever touch your heart and soul...*

Her knees threatened to give out, her body sagging. Rafe supported her with his body, bracing one brawny forearm around her middle as Dominic moved lower, his dark head trailing down from her breast, moving past Rafe's arm to press a hot, openmouthed kiss against her navel.

Jerking on the cuffs, she opened and closed her hands, desperate to touch, to grab and hold. Then Dominic spread the folds of her pussy with his fingers and pushed his tongue inside her. The devilish stroke of his tongue, the cool press of his fangs against her, and she exploded, bucking against his mouth in one fast, hard, furious climax.

Rafe chuckled behind her, sliding his free hand up her side, cupping her breast, teasing her still-damp nipple as he murmured, "Jumping the gun a little, aren't ya, Belle?"

She couldn't answer. Even though she didn't need to breathe, she still felt out of breath, her mind blurring.

"She's got the sweetest pussy," Dominic muttered, sitting back on his heels, staring up at her. His eyes looked almost drugged. "How can you taste so damned sweet?"

Rafe's lips moved at her temple as he whispered, "You call to him... That sweet, powerful vampire magick, woman's magick. It's inside you, driving us both insane."

Against her backside, she felt the hard length of Rafe's cock, still covered by the black cloth of his trousers. Shifting a little, she trailed her fingers up his length. "Turnabout is fair play," she said softly as another tremor racked her body. Rafe's hands on her loosened and she slid out of his hold, moving a few feet away, spinning around to stare at them.

Wetting her lips with her tongue, she whispered softly, "Get nekkid...I want to look at both of you."

Dominic's hands moved to his clothes, tugging and tearing at them while Rafe shrugged out of his coat, the heavy leather falling to the floor with a muffled thud. Dominic's shirt went flying across the room and Sheila took a step toward him, eyeing the smooth, muscled length of his chest.

Movement from Rafe drew her eyes and she felt her heart slam into her ribs as his shirt fell from his fingertips. His hands went to his belt buckle, loosening it. As he unzipped his pants, Sheila whispered, "Sweet mercy."

Maybe vampires *could* have heart attacks. She couldn't remember her heart ever beating this hard...had she ever felt it pound like this?

Her head was spinning, and she felt dizzy. She couldn't figure out what she was to look at—Rafe's cock as it sprang free from his trousers or Dominic as he shucked his shoes and reached for the zipper of his jeans.

Rafe was naked first. Crossing to him, she rose on her toes to press her lips to his. That hard, firm mouth opened and she pushed her tongue greedily inside, whimpering as he bit her lightly and his hands came up to cup her hips. Her breasts flattened against his chest—one knee pushed between her thighs, moving upward until she was riding the muscled length, his hands dragging her back and forth.

Behind her, she felt the warmth from Dominic's body moving closer and when he pressed against her from behind, cuddling his cock against her ass, she trembled.

Her head was spinning. Wrenching her mouth away from Rafe's, she squirmed between them until they each backed up, letting her move a little. They had too much control over this situation and she had none. Too damn much. She sucked air into her lungs and the cool air helped clear her head a little.

"Sheila?"

Rafe's voice was soft, a little concerned. Keeping her eyes down, she sucked in another breath of air, focusing on the calming action. She may not need the air, but there was something in that simple gesture that helped her push the cloud of lust aside so she could think a little.

Slowly, she lifted her eyes and studied Rafe's cock. The vein along the underside of it throbbed under her watchful gaze. A clear bead of fluid gathered on the crest, beckoning to her. Sinking to her knees, she traced the tip of her tongue over him, taking that salty drop inside her mouth, relishing it before sliding her mouth up and down his length.

Rafe groaned, a deep harsh sound that made satisfaction roll through her. With slow precision, she sucked him. When his hands came up to cup her head, trying to force her to take him faster, she bit down warningly with her teeth. His hands fell away as he whispered, "Fuck, Sheila."

Sitting back on her heels, she stared up at him with a slow smile, wiggling her wrists to make the cuffs jingle musically. "Take them off, Rafe," she whispered.

His fangs had dropped again, the tips sliding down, glinting in the light as he snarled at her. Lowering her head again, she licked a slow path down his balls and repeated, "Take them off."

He moved away from her so fast, she never even saw him go. Sliding her eyes to the left, she sat back on her heels and stared at Dominic. His eyes were on her breasts and she looked down, a slow smile spreading across her face as she saw how her bound position forced her breasts upward and out.

"Come here, Dominic."

Dominic's eyes moved to her face and she cocked her head at him, smiling. Rafe stood behind her now, and she felt the tremor of his hands as he messed with the cuffs. Dominic moved slowly to stand in front of her, one hand wrapped loosely around his erection.

She took his cock in her mouth, taking him inside with one long, slow stroke. His taste was different from Rafe's, salty, his skin not as warm. He tasted of the ocean, she thought, sliding her lips back up his length before moving forward again, not stopping until she felt his cock bump against the back of her throat. Dominic's breath hissed out, and his hands came up, cupping her head, fingers tangling in her hair.

The cuffs fell away from one wrist and she brought her hands forward, not worrying about the other cuff that braceleted her right wrist. One hand slid up Dominic's thigh, her fingers stroking over his sac while she reached behind her with the other hand.

Rafe's hand caught hers and she pulled him forward, shifting her attention to the thicker length of his cock, licking on him like an ice-cream cone while she wrapped the fingers of her free hand around Dominic's length, pumping up and down.

Harsh groans filled the air and she could feel the fine trembling of their bodies. Sitting back, she smiled up at them. Fair play, she thought.

That was her last clear thought, because Rafe pounced on her, slanting his mouth across hers as he took her to the floor, stretching her hands over her head as he plunged his tongue into her mouth. The cool black tile bit into her back, a startling contrast to Rafe's warm, sleekly muscled body. His cock pressed against her belly as one knee pushed between her thighs, pressing upward so he could stroke it over the pad of her pussy.

Then he was gone, her body cold in the air and clamoring for him.

Dominic knelt at her side and she rolled toward him, cupping one hand over the back of his neck and drawing his mouth toward hers. As he met her lips, she pushed him backward and he went. Covering his body with hers, she teased herself by rubbing the wet folds of her pussy against his cock, shifting so that she could rub her clit against him.

Dominic growled at her and one big hand came up, cupping her hip and holding her still. Rising, she stared down at him, her body shuddering. She watched as he wrapped a hand around his cock, urging her upward so that she could take him inside. A hungry little mewl slipped from her and she shifted, moving so that the tip of his cock was poised at her entrance.

"Fuck her, Dominic."

Both of them turned as one to stare at Rafe as he strode back across the room. In his hand, he held a blue plastic bottle and Sheila's excitement careened higher as she realized what it was. She didn't know for sure where the lube had come from, but maybe the club provided it.

Handy…very handy.

Dragging her eyes up, she met his, terror and anticipation twining inside her. Maybe a little *too* handy.

His lips crooked in a teasing smile and he knelt beside her, stroking one hand down her ass. "Now you didn't think you were going to leave here without fucking both of us, did you? He's too hot, burning for you…if you walked away from him without letting him put that fire out, he'd snap." His eyes never left hers as he leaned forward, pressing his lips against her shoulder before he again said to Dominic, "Fuck her."

Something rolled through the air, a power she wasn't unfamiliar with…a Master speaking, commanding. The reservations she had felt withered away and died and she screamed abruptly as Dominic gripped her hips and buried his cock inside her.

Dominic's eyes were wide and blind, his teeth bared as he threw his head back. The cords in his neck stood out and Sheila fell forward, licking at his neck, raking her teeth along his skin as his cock shuttled in and out of her aching pussy.

She was aware of Rafe moving behind her and she whimpered as she felt him kneeling down behind her, his cock against her backside, his hands stroking up and down her back, one finger trailing down the seam of her ass.

As if they had rehearsed this act a thousand times, Dominic slowed his frantic thrusts as Rafe applied the lubricant to her puckered anus. He pushed inside with his finger and crooned softly to her. Then he pushed a second finger in, pumping in and out slowly.

Catching her lip between her teeth, she arched, pain streaking through her. It had been too long since she had done this...not since she had kicked Rafe out of her bed, and her muscles were tense, too tense and damn it, she couldn't...

Lifting her head, she turned to look at Rafe with wide, panicked eyes. "Rafe, I can't..." she wailed.

His hand came up, cupping over the back of her neck, urging her back down. Dominic's mouth took hers, his hands cupping her face as he stroked his tongue inside her mouth, falling into a slow tantalizing rhythm. His hips circled against hers teasingly and she gasped as the friction again lit the fires inside her. Her clit ached — a visceral, needy ache.

Rafe started to fuck her ass with his fingers, his other hand stroking over the full globes, sliding up and down her spine, gliding upward to cup one breast in his hand.

They fucked her into a frenzy and she erupted around Dominic with a scream, quivering as Dominic scraped his teeth over her neck, breaking the surface and licking the deep wine-red blood from her flesh.

Everything seemed to freeze, though, as Rafe moved closer, his fingers withdrawing from the tight clasp of her ass, only to be replaced by the blunt tip of his cock.

She arched up as he pushed inside, slowly, working past the tight ring of muscle there. With slow, shallow strokes, he pushed her back into ecstasy, waiting until she started to push back against him before he thrust deeper.

She wailed out his name and collapsed against Dominic, her breasts flattening against his chest, their hearts banging against each other. "Rafe..."

He heard the soft, helpless whimper and it just made him hotter, made him harder. He stared down, watching the pink moue of her ass flower open around his cock, taking him inside slowly.

Through the thin membrane, he could feel Dominic's cock, throbbing and jerking in the snug confines of Sheila's pussy. "She's got the sweetest pussy, doesn't she?" Rafe said gruffly, flicking his eyes upward to meet Dominic's gaze.

The younger man looked drugged, his eyes wide and dark, the flickering glow of vampire starting to emerge. "Fuck, yeah," Dominic groaned.

The need to move, to come, was heavy on Dominic, Rafe could feel it. Sliding just a little inside the younger man's control, he reined in the pulsating need to come as he whispered against Sheila's ear, "Ride him while I ride you."

Her hips rolled forward, then back, and Rafe hissed as the motion took another inch of his cock inside her ass. "You're tight," he whispered, hunkering over her, pushing deeper, limiting how much she could move. "You feel it?"

Sheila whimpered as she rocked her hips again, still moving slowly. It took him deeper, then she slid away to take Dominic fully inside.

"You feel it?" he repeated. "Tell me what you feel...what you want..."

Sheila's voice shook as she whispered, "It feels hot...tight...too much..."

Rafe gritted his teeth—she flexed around him, the silken, clinging muscles of her ass caressing his length. "And what do you want?"

"Damn it, Rafe," she snarled, shoving back against him as much as she could. He grinned wickedly as she demanded, "Fuck me, damn it. Both of you..."

The words ended in a wail as Rafe started to plunge, hard and deep. Beneath Sheila, Dominic bucked, and Rafe could feel him pumping against her, inside her, as well. Dimly, he was aware of Dominic's hands coming up to grip at Sheila's waist, bracing her weight just slightly, keeping her from collapsing against him under Rafe's plundering cock.

Pulling back, he stared down at her, where he entered her, just the head of his cock still inside her. Savagely, he pushed back inside, fucking her hard, deep, forcing her to take his cock and feeling her erupt around him, screaming his name.

Sharply, he barked out, "Dominic, don't come. Not yet."

Sheila sobbed as the climax racked her body. Dominic muttered, "Shit. I gotta come...she's too hot, oh hell..."

Rafe ordered, "Don't!"

He felt the power that flooded the room, dimly aware that it was him, asserting his dominance over the younger vampire, but more...he was aware of Sheila's whimpering pleas, the way her skin started to flush, the way she bucked under his hands.

Slowing his thrusts, he moved seductively within her, waiting until she had calmed, feeling Dominic follow his lead.

"Suck on her nipples, Dom," he whispered, wrapping one forearm around her limp body and lifting her for the other man. "She tastes sweet...hot...like strawberries just pulled off the summer vines."

Turning his head, he stared at their reflections in the mirror, Sheila's long banner of golden curls spilling down her back, around her shoulders, blocking his view. Reaching up, he pushed her hair aside and watched Dominic suck one nipple deep inside his mouth.

Sheila's head hung limply, her eyes closed, her mouth open as another soft moan slid from her.

As Dominic pulled back, her nipple, deep pink and hard, wet from Dominic's mouth, gleamed in the light. Sliding his hand up her side, Rafe cupped her breast in his hand, plucking on her nipple and feeling her clench around his cock in reaction.

"Tell me you love me," he whispered, hunkering down over her, resting his chin on the curve of her shoulder and watching as another man loved her body.

Her eyes fluttered open and she shifted, staring at him blindly. She shuddered and Rafe smelled blood, dropping his eyes to see Dominic licking a drop of blood away from the swell of her breast. Hunger flared inside him. Cupping her chin in his hand, he arched her neck, licking the skin he'd exposed and whispering against it, "Tell me."

"I love you...so much it hurts," she gasped.

Rafe sank his teeth into her skin and felt her start to come around them, her anal muscles clenching at his cock.

Her pussy would be hot, tight, the muscles inside her clinging to Dominic as he thrust inside her.

Her blood flowed down his throat like wine — fuck her, or feed…damn it… Lifting his head, he licked the small wounds on her neck before he straightened and started to plunge his dick inside her. Dropping the reins of control, he felt Dominic react. He could feel the other man as he bucked and plunged, his breath rattling harshly in the air.

As Sheila wailed out his name, Rafe came, the semen jetting from his cock in scalding bursts. His head fell back, and he stared blindly at the ceiling as he whispered, "I love you, Belle."

* * * * *

Dominic curled against Sheila from behind now, the scent of soap clinging to their bodies. Across the room, he could see the humans they had fed from, sleeping, still oblivious, sprawled on some enormous padded cushion Rafe had tossed on the floor.

Dominic didn't remember that. Or where the cushion had come from…hell, he barely remembered the shower, or Sheila kneeling in front of him and taking him in her mouth, sucking him off, giving him yet another mind-blowing orgasm while Rafe fucked her pussy from behind.

Part of him felt guilty.

It should be wrong, taking the blood, using them that way…right?

But another part of him felt a satisfaction so enormous, so complete, it encompassed his entire being.

But he was jealous.

Sheila draped against Rafe's body, her fingers trailing up and down his chest and via the mirror overhead, he could see the small smile on her face.

Rafe's eyes were closed, but he had the same smile, satisfied...complete. He'd known when he first started pursuing the sad-eyed blonde that she had somebody in her heart. Normally it was a very bad idea, pursuing a woman on the rebound. He just hadn't been able to help himself.

Of course, if he had known where he'd end up—a vampire, condemned to walk in darkness for years and years to come—well, hell. Maybe he still would have done it.

He didn't know, but there was something about this that felt fated. Like he was destined to come into this life.

He wanted to kill the bastard who had done this to him. The memories came at him in the bitter dark of his sleep, making him scream silently, making him want to beg for mercy. And that totally pissed him off.

But that wasn't exactly why he wanted that man dead.

He wanted him dead to save others from his fate...not being a vampire, but the...the rape.

His body stiffened as he admitted it silently to himself.

He'd been raped. Hell, being raped hadn't even been one of his worst nightmares... It was beyond that, something that had been incomprehensible for him, something unthinkable. And now it haunted him. He wanted to get strong, stronger than he was...strong enough to keep this from happening ever again.

Strong enough to protect others.

Maybe that would help fill the sick hole that had taken root in his gut.

"You're thinking too hard, Dom," Sheila murmured sleepily.

Stroking a hand down her hip, he pressed his lips against her shoulder. "Sorry, sugar. Just got a busy mind."

Damn, would it sound ridiculous if he said "thank you"? His mind was busy, all right. Whirling, full of relief and satisfaction—this was the first time he'd felt like a man since that night. Even though just a few days had passed, his entire life had changed. When it had happened, a sick fear had settled in him. He'd wondered if he would feel so scared all his life? So broken? Wondered if he would ever feel like a man again.

He doubted Rafe or Sheila could understand how deep that fear had run. Doubted they could understand what it had meant to him to feel a woman sighing under his hands, to feel her come around his cock, and to come inside her.

God above, how could one night so totally destroy the fabric of his soul?

Dominic didn't realize he had whispered that part aloud until Rafe shifted up onto his elbow, and stared at him with black eyes. "He didn't destroy you, Dominic. You're stronger than that. And now even stronger than before. Swords forged in fire and all that."

Dominic flushed, the blood that pumped so sweetly through his veins just moments before rushing to stain his cheeks.

Sheila wiggled between them, rolling over onto her side, wrapping an arm around him. "Busy thoughts, huh?" she whispered, hugging him tightly. "You're going to be fine, Dominic. I don't know what is running through your head, but I see pain in your eyes. Feel it in the air around you...but it will pass. Whatever he did to you, you're stronger than that."

Staring into her compassionate blue eyes, Dominic felt the fear festering in him finally break loose, leaping to his lips before he could stop it. "What if I become a monster like he is?" he asked harshly, rising up, closing his fingers around her arms, staring at her desperately.

"Shhh," she whispered, pressing her fingers to his lips. "You've already chosen your path, Dom. Even if you haven't acknowledged it, we know. You're one of us, you'll fight and destroy men like him, not become one."

"How do you know?" he demanded, unaware of the torment written all over his face. Just aware of that sick fear in his gut...what if he did became a monster?

Glancing down, he realized with shock that his hold had turned bruising on her arms, the flesh above and below his grip turning white. Disgusted with himself, he let go of her, and started to turn away, only to have her arms come up around him. One hand buried in his hair, the other stroked up and down his back.

"I just know." Her lips skimmed across his cheek and she shifted back, still holding him close but staring into his eyes. "Dominic, I've been a vampire for more than twenty years, and a Hunter for fifteen. I know what evil is, I know its taint, its taste, how it feels. I know what it looks like when it lurks inside a man's eyes." A slow smile curved her lips as she gazed into his eyes, stroking her fingers down his cheek. "You're many things, Dominic, but evil isn't one of them."

Squeezing his eyes closed, he rested his forehead against hers, wrapping his arms around her. She shifted into his lap, her naked hip pressing against his cock. Blood stirred and he felt his cock lengthen, harden. But he was just content to sit there holding her.

Feeling Rafe's eyes on him, he looked up, meeting the older vampire's dark gaze. "I needed this," Dominic said quietly. It was the closest he could come to voicing what was in his heart.

Rafe's mouth crooked in a wry grin. "Yeah. I kinda guessed that." He sank down behind Sheila, pressing his lips to her shoulder. She squirmed a little and shifted until she could wrap an arm around Rafe's waist as well. "I think we all did."

Some twenty minutes later, they prepared to leave the room, gathering clothes, and shoes. Dominic helped Sheila find her purse as Rafe woke both Beth and Jake, staring into their eyes for long moments.

Finding the palm-sized purse under the bed, she slid the strap across her chest, and then leaned over to whisper to Dominic, "He's leaving a false memory. As far as they are concerned, we all had a major gangbang in here."

Sheila's heart smiled as Dominic flashed her a wicked grin, the humor she adored lurking in his eyes. His black brows arched over his dark eyes and he whispered, "You mean we didn't?"

Flashing a flirtatious smile at him, she said, "Well, maybe we did. But they weren't involved. Now they don't feel so shortchanged."

Dominic slid his eyes to the two humans who stood staring at Rafe as though they were entranced. Well, they were, sort of, lost in his eyes as he created the false memory of a wild, wicked night. "Something tells me a memory instead of the real thing is shortchanging them."

Sheila snorted. "Not for her. She isn't going to find what she is looking for with him. He's no more a master than I am."

Rafe turned away from the humans as they sank together onto the bed, their eyes staring sightlessly at them. "Well, not that I'm welling to turn sub on you, but I'd sure as hell love to see you in leather and stilettos," he murmured, moving closer and pulling her against him.

Waggling her brows, she teased, "You got it. So long as I get to see you in leather pants, chest bare, and some kinky black leather collar with studs on it."

They felt it, then. The presence of a deadly evil drifting through the air.

Searching.

The spit dried in Sheila's mouth as she cuddled against Rafe's chest, fear rolling through her as that presence tried to reach out and touch her.

Rafe pressed his lips to her brow and then he moved her protectively behind him. Dominic moved to stand at Rafe's side—Sheila realized that Dominic would to be a Master at some point, just by that simple, courteous action. Moving to stand between a woman and harm seemed like such a simple thing—but weaker vampires would have felt as devastated and weakened by that presence as Sheila did.

She swallowed, dragging her tongue across her dry lips, focusing on the back of Rafe's head, on the unique, male scent of him, anything to keep that fog of fear from taking control of her mind.

As she fell whimpering to the floor, she never even realized how tight the vampire's hold had become around her.

* * * * *

Rafe heard her fall, felt her fall. If the strength of a person's heart and soul determined who would be Master, then he knew she would have stood against any and all enemies.

But the evil felled her.

However, both Rafe and Dominic stood in the face of it. Rafe felt a strength inside him unlike any he had ever felt before. It felt…solid. Clean. Real.

The land.

It was coming from the very land beneath the foundation of the club, in the air around them. Drawing on it, he forced a shield between Sheila and the presence that had flooded the room.

It had no voice, no face, no name…but he knew who it was. It was the man he was going to kill.

All of them felt the summons as the vampire tried to lure Sheila to him.

Rafe cut his eyes to her and then lifted his gaze to Dominic. Dominic understood the wordless command and he moved to hunker protectively at Sheila's side, whispering in her ear, crooning to her. As some small part of Sheila heard him, he felt the very strength of her spirit flood her soul and she shoved the chains of fear off.

Calmly, Rafe said, "You trespass. This land, this woman…they are mine."

A low chuckle floated through the air. "So…a Master has come to claim the land I call home."

Rafe snorted, flicking his hair out of his eyes. It was somewhat discomfiting, talking to an enemy who had no face, yet hearing the voice echo all around them, like it came from everywhere.

But he didn't let that show by his expression as he replied, "You call the land home, perhaps. But it doesn't claim you. This earth knows its Master." His lips crooked up in a cocky grin as he added, "And it ain't you."

Malevolent laughter filled the air. "And I assume you think it is you?"

Rafe chuckled. "What do you think?" He cast Dominic a look, then smiled gently at Sheila. "This woman's Master is miles away, states away. She, understandably, has less strength to stand alone against one such as you. But…well, I stand. As does my lieutenant." Okay, well, Dominic might not be a lieutenant, but he was definitely one of Rafe's.

His first. A slow smile spread over Rafe's lips as he realized that.

There was a silence, a stillness, like the calm before the storm. And then the rage struck. Pummeling the air around Rafe like a fist. Rafe just stood there, never blinking.

Sheila's breath shuddered out of her in a soft, shaky sigh, but her mind and will were still her own. He felt her fear, her anger, *her*. Dominic crouched on the ground beside her, hugging her protectively against him.

Then the true storm hit, far more powerful than that first wave of fear, arrowing toward Dominic with focused intent.

"This one is mine…I tasted of his blood and flesh long before you saw him, Hunter. I shall take what is mine."

That low urging came again, like a tractor beam, unseen but felt as it swept the room. It rolled off of Rafe, and it couldn't work on Sheila unless she let the fear overtake her. With Dominic's help, with Rafe's presence, it was easier to fight. Only her Master could summon her, and Eli was nowhere around.

But Dominic...Rafe held himself ready to lunge for the young vampire if he had to.

The sweeping call suddenly erupted into a vicious wave of power, more like a hurricane than anything and wind whipped through the room, the storm swelling into a crescendo then dying away.

"He is mine! I know his taste, his blood..."

Rafe merely blinked. "He lay dying. Another's blood gave him the strength to hang on, but it was my blood, my power that brought him back. He is mine. Not yours."

Now Rafe's power tore free, his own rage slipping to the fore. His lips peeled back from his fangs as he snarled, "Face me *now*...or get the fuck away from me and mine."

* * * * *

Sheila's chest felt tight.

If she was still human, she would have thought it was from the breath she'd been holding.

But she thought it was fear — maybe it was actually fear that made a human's chest tighten until even breathing was agony. Maybe that's what it was, not how they held their breath.

He was gone. The only thing left of him as they moved through the night toward their home was the fear that clung to her skin like a glove.

How had he done that?

179

Rafe was only a couple of hundred years old. This bastard they were after, this faceless Pierre, was centuries older.

She didn't want to ask, though.

Hell, she wasn't sure she *could* ask. At this point, she was afraid if she tried to talk little more than babbling would leave her mouth.

Sweet heaven, the fear…she hadn't ever felt anything like that. It had rolled across her skin and pooled in her throat, choking her. How had Rafe and Dominic stood still in the face of it? Especially Dominic…he was just days old.

For once, Sheila found herself lacking. She hadn't the strength it took to stand so easily in the face of fear. It wasn't often she doubted her worth, doubted her ability. But now, she did.

A vampire, days old, had stood strong in the face of a demonically evil bastard and she had fallen to the floor sobbing.

She studied Dominic from the corner of her eye. That Rafe had stood, well, it had surprised her, but just a little. Rafe was a powerful bastard. He had a compelling way about him—he'd had it for as long as she had known him. She suspected it had been there for decades longer than that. She'd never mentioned it, but even Eli hadn't been able to compare to what she had sensed within Rafe.

But Dominic…how had he done it? Was he going to be that powerful?

He still wasn't at full strength. So how…

Maybe it was Rafe. Vampires often took on many of the attributes of their first meal…shit.

Rafe hadn't exactly been the first meal. A vampire's blood could sustain another weaker vampire for a short time, and it was sweet, heaven above knew. A Master's blood could bind lesser vampires, bring them back from the brink, like Rafe had done with Dominic. A blood bond between Master and servant saw to it that the lesser vampire stayed at his Master's side

But after a time, a vampire's blood was...hell. Cotton candy. All fluff, no substance. A Master's blood had more kick to it, and also provided nourishment...for a time, but only a time.

So, then...Robbie.

Had Robbie's blood done this?

The blood of a powerful witch, even one who was as simple as Robbie, perhaps... Sheila mused over that. Better to dwell on that than her fear. Vampires tended to take on some of the traits from the first person who supplied the blood after they changed.

A person with no magick couldn't take on the magical aspects of a witch, although perhaps they could learn to withstand some of the darker magicks that worked on emotions. That was what a vampire's weapon of fear was. They were able to prey on the emotions of fear and terror.

Had Robbie passed some odd immunity to the fear to Dominic?

Maybe more...there was a strong heart within Robbie. A strong soul. The heart and soul of a man who would have been a force to be reckoned if he hadn't been born the way he had.

Then Sheila felt shame move through her.

Robbie had an innocence to him, a purity that wouldn't have survived all the long years he'd lived if he had been born whole.

* * * * *

Ella was dozing, curled up on her little bed, feeling the warmth of the fire on her face, the brilliant blaze making a flickering light show even behind her closed lids.

Warm, secure, almost happy…that was how it found her.

The dark nasty maw of power that slid over her, pulling at her.

"Ahhh…it is you…"

Terror locked her limbs. She couldn't move, couldn't do any more than wheeze out a terrified breath as her lids opened. Searching in the dark, she couldn't see him, but his voice…she'd heard his voice.

"Come to me, little pet. It's time to play…"

Ella whimpered, shaking her head as she tried to inch back, as though she could somehow move away from the voice that had slid inside her mind.

"None of that, pet. I've had enough impudence tonight. *Come!*"

Slowly, she slid from the bed, unaware that Robbie had woken from sleep, and rose from the cot across the room to stare at her with dark, worried eyes.

As she followed the summons, she felt as though she was a dark, mindless pit of despair. Helpless to do anything but follow.

Robbie followed her out, his jaw clenched, his hands closed into loose fists at his side.

The bad man…

* * * * *

Rafe and Sheila slid inside the dark little house where Ella and Robbie lived, following Dominic's back through the shadows.

None of them had spoken more than a handful of words since they had left the club.

None really knew what to say.

Tonight was the night.

Sheila was questioning that she had done the right thing, staying. She was no match against that vampire.

Dominic didn't think of that. Instead, he simply drifted, his thoughts floating from the time when he and Rafe had pressed Sheila's sweet, soft body between them, to the hot splash of blood in his belly as he fed from the woman — thinking on nothing and everything all at once.

Rafe brooded.

So caught up in their own thoughts, none of them saw Leandra as she rose from her crouched position by the fire.

She had to clear her throat to catch their attention and when they turned to stare at her, they all felt a chill run through at the grim look on her face. "Dey are gone."

Sheila started, blinked slowly, then turned her head to look around the small room. "Gone?" she asked quietly.

Leandra arched a brow. "Gone. I felt something lingering in de air when I got here a little while ago, but it faded too fast for me to track it. The little vampire and Robbie, dey are gone."

Rafe snarled, spinning away from Leandra. The tips of his fangs had slid out past his upper lip and his eyes were glowing and hot.

"Almost dawn, mon," Leandra said quietly. "Ya can't be goin' out now, dis close to the sun."

Rafe's hand closed over the doorknob, but even as she spoke, they all felt it. The ever-brightening sky overhead, the sun as it first slid over the horizon.

"Fuck!" Rafe ground out, pressing his forehead against the door.

Sheila moved up, reaching out to touch his shoulder but he spun away, avoiding her touch as he started to pace, swearing under his breath.

They all felt his anger, but only Leandra understood how deep it ran, and that he was angry at himself. She felt the same way. "We will go after dem…once we rest. And we must wait until the sun isn't so strong—then we will go."

"That may be too late," Rafe growled.

Leandra lifted one shoulder. "I don't tink so, Rafe. He rests too…most of us cannot fight the urge to rest during the day. Even Malachi sleeps while the sun drifts in the sky. And he doesn't have to. It's instinct. And this man, he is arrogant. He will sleep, tinking none of us dare to face him. I know spells dat will protect from the sun. We use those and den, while he still sleeps, we go. We find him." An evil light lit her eyes. "I'll get out Robbie and the little vampire, den we barbecue…"

Chapter Eight

Barbecue…

Robbie thought about that as he followed Ella.

She was gone from his sight. Soon as she got out of the house, she'd started to run.

But he could follow her. Robbie could feel her inside him and he knew he could find Ella even if she left the world.

In his heart, he always knew where to find her.

So he moved through the streets, thinking about what Leandra had said. He liked her.

She was strong. She was pretty. And she was filled with a light so deep and true blue, it almost hurt to look at her. And she was smart. A barbecue.

If he killed Pierre, they were all safe.

He was good with fire.

Robbie liked to play with it. That was the reason his father's tribe had forced him to leave, because he liked playing with fire so much. They'd tried to cure him, making him fast and serve the holy man for years and years, but still, he'd always sneak off to play with the fire.

He hadn't meant to catch that white man's lone, empty cabin on fire. But after he'd done it, even though he'd stopped the fire before it could spread, his people had made him leave.

After that, there was loneliness. Robbie had no idea how much time passed between him leaving his father's people, and Pierre taking him. He remembered wide open and empty land under the burning hot scorch of the summer sun, and then there were trains, loud smelly trains, then more towns, more people…then Pierre had come.

After they'd gotten away from him, the land had changed even more. Silver things moved through the air, and there were smaller boxes, like the trains, not as loud, but still smelly. And they traveled in packs on the roads.

But it wasn't so bad.

Ella was with him.

So long as he had Ella… A smile spread across his face as he followed her scent. At the end of the long, dark road, he could see her. Finally. She had slowed down, and Robbie saw the long, silvery-yellow hair that hung almost to her hips.

He liked seeing it blowing in the breeze…he liked…

Pain!

It cut across him like fire and he fell to his knees, gasping for air, his hands clutching at his belly to find what was trying to cut his gut out.

Nothing…nothing…but when he opened his eyes, it was not the gravel road that he saw under his knees. It was a dark carpet that was getting darker as he looked. And Ella—her banner of hair spread around her head, while she clutched at her belly. Blood spilled through her hands, dark blackish-purple blood, and darker things…

"Ella," he whispered, huddling on the ground, wrapping his arms around his knees as power whispered through the air. *Don't let it see me…*

It drifted on past him and he felt a whimper building in his throat as he continued to stare at the ground, but saw Ella instead. They'd cut her open.

A growl rumbled in his throat as he heard the ghost of laughter, laughter he hadn't heard in years. Rising, he stared through the darkness at the house that loomed in front of him.

"You cut her open," he said hotly, unaware that his eyes had started to glow.

He felt Ella start as he moved toward the house. "Robbie…"

"Hush, Ella. It's my turn now," he said quietly as he started to circle around the house.

There were vampires in there.

Just vampires. Pierre, some others he didn't know, though he felt the darkness of their hearts.

He hunkered down outside the house, sliding his eyes to the eastern sky.

He might be dumb, but he wasn't totally stupid. He knew vampires. They slept during the day, even Pierre.

And day was coming fast.

Ella was hurting some, but already her vampire body was healing the injury. Pierre had done it to hurt, not to kill and he didn't care if she healed a little. She was his puppy, his toy…

Robbie could feel his thoughts. Almost hear them, like a radio — *the big idiot who always follows you? Is he with you?* Pierre demanded, kneeling beside her, tracing a finger through the blood.

She didn't answer, just focused on directing her energy to heal the hole in her belly.

Pierre didn't seem to care. At all. He rose, kicking Ella in the side, and Robbie had to fight not to run to the house as the bastard just turned around and walked away, leaving Ella curled up and whimpering from the pain of the kick.

Robbie silently mouthed, "Barbecue." And his hands began to glow.

* * * * *

Sheila cast a nervous look at the sun shining down through the cover of clouds. Even though those clouds were a fragile shield, she hoped they held.

The sun peeked out from behind them, never shining fully on them, and Sheila pretended that made all the difference in the world.

Oh, she knew it didn't.

Sunlight was sunlight, and if it struck her, she was dead.

But the spell from Leandra glittered around her like a fine cape, protecting her body, just barely visible if Sheila stared at her skin long enough—there and then gone.

Rafe turned his beloved Bel Air over to Leandra without blinking, and Sheila briefly entertained the thought that Leandra had cast another spell, all on Rafe. But the idea was gone before it really formed.

As they drove through the burning light of day, she stared at the clouds almost hypnotized. "It's so blue," she whispered softly.

Dominic sat in the backseat next to her, his arms folded across his chest, his eyes scrunched tightly closed. "Dom, don't you want to see it?"

He shook his head and said, "Why? To remind me I may never see it again?"

Sheila laid her palm against the glass, watching as they passed by a big yellow bus on the street, a small girl rising up onto her knees to wave at her. Sheila waved back, feeling a tear trickle down her cheek.

"I don't know…maybe to help you understand why we do it."

She watched the school bus disappear behind them and then she turned around in her seat, feeling the sun shining down on her flesh through the window. "Maybe to help remind us why we do it…we see only our world after we've been in the dark so long. Seeing the light helps us remember."

They left the city, following the Sam Cooper Boulevard out of town, then turning off and taking first one turn, and then another, another until trees closed around them and the road turned to gravel.

"We get out here," Leandra said quietly, slowing the car to a stop and turning it off, tossing the keys to Rafe.

As Sheila climbed from the car, her entire body was shaking.

* * * * *

Robbie moved through the halls, searching for signs of life. All the vampires slept. Ella…where was Ella?

Where had they taken her?

He was so focused on finding her…he almost didn't feel them come.

Sheila. He could feel her. A warm, sweet touch on his soul as he focused on her.

Leandra, Rafe, Dominic…they were here. Robbie wasn't surprised. Leandra, she was…cool. He'd heard the word before and he liked it. Leandra was cool. Some people might think she was scary, and Robbie had…at first. Then he saw her, looked into her sad eyes and felt her soul.

She wasn't scary.

She was scared. But she faced that fear.

Robbie could do that too. And he would.

If he hadn't been focusing on them, he might have seen Pierre in time.

But instead, he barely realized the vampire had moved out of a room, until he heard Ella's soft gasp.

Turning, he faced Pierre, his jaw clenched as he stared at Ella and watched as Pierre shoved her to the ground.

"My pets are back," Pierre whispered. His eyes widened as he studied Robbie and he smiled, a slow, nasty smile that made Robbie's skin crawl. "And this one has developed some teeth."

Robbie felt everything inside him clench, his skin felt tight and hot, and he started to see red. "Get away from her."

Pierre just laughed.

"You won't hurt her again!" Robbie snarled, moving toward Pierre.

Pierre laughed, a low, warm sound that made Robbie's belly twist painfully, and vomit rise in his throat.

"Oh, you're right…after this, she hurts no more." Two vampires came out of the darkness and grabbed Robbie's arms. They slowed him down. But they didn't stop him.

He was still too late though.

He reached Ella just as Pierre dropped to his knees by her side, smiling at Robbie all the while.

He smiled when he stroked a hand down Ella's slender neck. Smiled as he closed his hand, his finger digging into her flesh...and smiled as he tore her throat out. "No more pain, pet. She's not worth the trouble," Pierre whispered, smiling brighter as he looked at Robbie.

Robbie screamed out her name and threw off the men holding his arms, falling to his knees as Pierre flung the bloody mess in his hand at Robbie. The gobs of flesh struck him in the chest, but Robbie barely noticed. Closing his hand around Ella's, he whispered her name, "Ella..."

She couldn't answer.

Blood was pouring from her neck in a gush and she stared up to his face. He felt her whisper his name in her mind as she faded away. Ella was weak. She couldn't live after losing that much blood. He knew that.

So he held her hand as she died, and when he lifted his face to stare at Pierre, he didn't realize the very fires of hell were burning in his dark eyes.

* * * * *

Leandra felt it, rolling across her skin like a nasty black wave.

Death... She hissed under her breath and turned to look at the others behind her. "Someting is wrong," she whispered hollowly.

Something soft, gentle drifted by them and Leandra felt her throat tighten as a sweet laugh sounded in the air.

A tear rolled down her cheek. "The little vampire... Ella...she's gone."

"No."

Sheila rasped out, shaking her head. *"No!"* She made a move to lunge for the house, but she didn't make it a foot before Rafe's hands closed over her arms.

At that second, the house exploded into a fireball.

And they all heard Robbie's soft voice, from everywhere, from nowhere, as he said, "Barbecue."

Several people tried to lunge from the lower floor of the house, but their bodies were nothing more than fireballs and they staggered just a few steps before they hit the ground and did nothing more than burn away to smoke and ash.

Sheila struggled against Rafe's hands, tears streaming down her cheeks. There were screams…people—no, vampires—still alive in there, screaming. And Robbie.

"Robbie!" she screamed, the pain rushing through her, hot and bitter. She kicked back at Rafe's legs and heard him grunt, but he didn't let go. "He's in there!"

Rafe pressed his lips against her brow. "Sheila, Belle, let him go… Ella's gone. He wants this…"

"He doesn't want to die!" she screamed.

"No. He wants to follow Ella," Rafe murmured. "Just like I'd follow you…let him go."

Horrendous cracks sounded, and then sparks shot up into the sky as the house collapsed in on itself. That last long, unearthly scream was silenced and then the fire stopped.

One minute there, and then it was gone, like a candle snuffed out.

"Shhh…"

They froze as they heard that voice, that gentle, deep voice. It drifted around them and Sheila gasped as something, a hand, brushed the tears away from her cheeks. "I'm going now. Ella is waiting."

And then he was gone.

There wasn't another living creature around, alive or undead.

All was silent.

Chapter Nine

Sheila stood at the door to Kelsey's house, staring at it numbly.

Rafe stood behind her, his hand resting on her shoulder as he stared up at the old, brownstone house. Sheila's hand closed around the doorknob, but instead of turning it, she just dropped her forehead against the smooth dark wood.

"It's over," she whispered thickly. "I don't understand. How can it be over…"

"Let's go inside, Belle," Rafe whispered, pressing his lips to her brow. "You need to rest."

She laughed bitterly. "Leandra didn't rest. She's already gone. Just smoke and ashes left of Ella and Robbie. They won't do anything but rest now," she whispered.

"They've earned it." Dominic stood behind them, staring at the sidewalk, shoulders slumped. Slowly, he lifted his head and stared at them. "They loved each other. But how could they do anything about it? They were unhappy, stuck in the lives they had."

His eyes were dark, bitter, but a smile appeared on his face as he spoke. "They aren't stuck anymore," he said quietly.

Those words circled through her head. *Not stuck anymore…* She remembered the way Robbie had looked at Ella, so openly adoring. How Ella took care of Robbie, and smiled when he was near.

And the sadness in the air. It was more than just fear. There was pain and frustration there as well. Sweet heaven, they had been a sad pair. A hopeless pair. What kind of happy ever after would they have…

Closing her eyes, she felt the hot tears trickle down her cheeks as she took a shaky breath. "You're right," she whispered, her voice tight and husky. Reaching up, she brushed away a tear as she repeated, "You're right. But damn it, it hurts."

Rafe's arms came around her, hugging her back against him, nuzzling her hair. "I know, pet. I know."

* * * * *

They stood on the porch for a long moment while Rafe stroked one hand up and down Sheila's arm soothingly.

Hours had passed.

They had searched through the rubble of the house briefly — until sirens wailed in the air, alerting them to the arrival of the fire department. Then the four of them had melted into the trees, watching from the shadows as the firefighters searched the ruin.

Nothing was found. The bodies of the vampires had burnt to nothing more than ashes. And after such a blaze, ashes were everywhere.

Robbie…she had no idea what had happened to the big witch's body. But the firefighters' search hadn't turned up any bodies. Leandra had searched, her amber eyes glinting with tears as she murmured, "I can find him…I can…"

Nothing.

Part of Rafe was bothered by that. They deserved —
something — though what, he didn't know.

But Dominic was right.

They had loved each other — a love that could never be
what it was truly meant to be.

And after so many years of suffering, of hiding, they
were free.

The moon drifted out from behind a wispy bank of
clouds, turning the dark edges of the cloud silver, shining
down on them. Turning Sheila's face up to him, he bussed
her mouth gently. "Let's go inside, Sheila. Let's go home."

She nodded, pushing the door open and stepping
inside, she turned back to smile at Rafe. "You know,
you've never been inside this house, slick."

A black brow arched and he drawled, "Really…and
that means…what?"

Snickering, she said, "I ought to *not* invite you in.
Make you suffer for a while."

Running his tongue over his teeth, he said, "I've
suffered enough."

Sheila leaned against the door, and a winsome smile
curved her pretty mouth up. Rafe felt a temporary
moment of panic — he wanted nothing more than to spend
the night loving that smooth, pale body. "I don't know —
six long months, I watched you walk around the Enclave,
never once looking at me, as though I no longer existed for
you. And before that…I only existed for you when you
wanted me."

Narrowing his eyes, he said, "Haven't we already
gotten past this?"

She chuckled. "Well, of course, we have. But I had to make you suffer a little," she whispered, pushing the door open wide. "Come inside, Rafe."

He crossed the threshold and hooked his hand behind her neck, pressing a rough, biting kiss to her mouth. He stilled at the sound of footsteps behind him. Lifting his head, he turned and saw Dominic walking back down the sidewalk, his dark head lowered, shoulders slumped.

"Where you going?"

Dominic stilled, flicking a glance at Rafe. "Home. It's been a while." His eyes darkened, a look of pain entered them and then he shrugged.

Rafe laughed. "Dom...this is home, don't you know that?"

Dominic turned back around, staring at Rafe, his eyes black in the night. They glittered in his solemn face and as Rafe came back outside, staring at Dominic, his body tensed.

Sheila followed him, moving to stand beside Rafe, reaching out and taking his hand in hers. "You know, don't you, that your old life...it's gone, right?" she asked gently when Rafe stood silent.

The young vampire flinched, his jaw clenching. Turning away, he hunched his shoulders as though he could block out the truth. "Yeah," he said roughly. "I know that. Shit...what in the hell am I supposed to do now? I've always known what I wanted—I can't do that now. Hell, I don't know *what* I am supposed to do."

Something inside Rafe's heart stirred...pity? His heart had been cold for so long, it was hard to always recognize the emotions stirring inside it. "I know."

Dominic's head raised, but he still stared out into the night. Bitterly, he asked, "Yeah? What?"

Sheila slid her hand from his and moved up to rest one hand lightly on Dominic's shoulder. "You're a Hunter...you're one of us, Dom. I knew that the minute I saw you lying in that bed. Come on...come inside...come home."

Dominic took the dark, drape-shrouded room under the stairs for that night.

Lori, or maybe Kelsey...one of the witches would come and lay the spells on the windows, spells that would protect the vampires from the sunlight that would drift in from time to time.

Maybe Kelsey would let them buy the house.

They needed a base, someplace to call home over the coming years as Rafe established his territory.

A big house...that more vampires, witches or weres would eventually call home.

This house, nestled on several acres on the outskirts of town would work wonderfully.

Sheila moved through, studying the rooms with an intensity she hadn't used before. On the third floor there was a room she'd fallen in love with, a pale ivory room with a magnificent four-poster canopy, high on a raised platform. But the windows—four of them—too much sunlight flooded the room.

They could close up one or two of those windows, maybe, cover the rest with thick drapes. Stroking one hand down the golden gleam of the comforter, she thought of sleeping here, in this big, golden bed, with Rafe next to her. A slow smile curved her lips and then she sighed, closing her hand into a fist.

"Pretty room," Rafe murmured neutrally from behind her.

Turning, she met his eyes and smiled, lifting one shoulder. "Yeah. I like it."

"Do you sleep in here?"

Sheila shook her head, hunching her shoulders at the thought of sleeping in a room not protected by sunlight, either by material substances or by magick. "No. The windows…" Lifting one shoulder, she said, "There's a bed below the stairs that I slept in. Dominic's down there. He needs more security from the sun than we do right now. The rest of the basement is empty."

Rafe came inside, sliding his hands into his back pockets.

The black shirt he wore was unbuttoned and it parted, revealing the hard muscles of his golden torso, that black line of hair that curled around his navel before disappearing inside his jeans. Her heart started to pound as she stared at him, gums aching as her fangs started to press against them.

"Couple of bedrooms," he murmured, circling around her, watching her closely. "We could take a mattress down to the basement come daybreak. Sleep there for now."

Sheila nodded, dragging her tongue across her lips as he passed in front of her, his upper arm brushing against her breasts as he continued to walk around her in a slow circle. Her nipples tightened into hard, demanding little peaks as he came to a halt behind her, gathering her hair in his fist and pulling it aside, baring her neck.

His tongue laved the skin there, one long, hot stroke before he raked his teeth across her skin. "But I don't want to sleep yet...not nearly yet," he purred.

Then he reached around her and cupped her breasts, kneading them with his palms, plumping them together, pinching her nipples—he played until she was rocking back against him and moaning.

"I love you..."

That low rough murmur, words she never thought she'd hear from him, sent a shiver down her spine and locked a fist around her heart. Covering his hands with hers, she pressed them against her flesh as she said softly, "I love you, too. Damn it, so much."

Rafe chuckled, sliding his hands from under hers and dropping to his knees, reaching around to open the snap at the waistband of the black fatigues she still wore. She looked down, watching as his hands took the black pants down her legs until they puddled around her ankles. His mouth, cool now, but so silky-soft, pressed against her ass, kissing one cheek, then the other.

"I adore you..."

Another kiss, pressed to the soft skin just above the crevice between her cheeks as he tugged her underwear down. "Worship you..."

One hand rested on her spine, pushing her upper body forward and down, until she was resting on the bed, her hips braced against the side. She quivered as his big hands came up and spread the cheeks of her ass, then his mouth pressed against the sensitive skin of her anus, his tongue gliding around it in one silken stroke.

"Need you," he breathed against her damp flesh, making her quiver.

Then he was gone and she heard the harsh grate of metal as he unzipped his clothes. His hands came back around her hips and she cast a look over her shoulder to see him pressing against her, his pants shoved down just far enough.

Sheila screamed as he shoved inside, her flesh still tight, unprepared. Digging her hands into the comforter, she hissed out, "Yes…"

He pulled out, his cock rasping against the soft tissues of her pussy, the flesh resisting him, squeezing him even as he withdrew. "You're not ready," he groaned, starting to pull away.

She shoved back against him, reaching back with one hand to grip his hip, to keep him from pulling away. "Don't stop," she whimpered. "I need this…need you…don't leave me."

"Never." His hands stroked over her ass, and he started to rock against her, slowly, and she felt the muscles in her pussy relax and open, the cream of her arousal wetting her inner folds.

"Harder, Rafe." Planting her hands on the bed, she shoved back against him and wiggled her ass. "Fuck me, damn it. Hard and fast and… *now!*"

The last word left her in a wail as he started to shaft her, pumping within her with hard, deep strokes, faster and faster until his flesh slapped against the taut skin of her buttocks.

She screamed as he pressed against the tight pucker of her ass with his thumb, the muscles there resisting him.

"You're tight," he whispered.

She shivered at the sound of his voice—deep, thick, drugged. He only sounded like that when he was very tired…or when he was deep inside her body. The sound of it caressed her flesh like a velvet glove, drawing her skin tighter, making her heart kick up until it felt as though her entire body felt its erratic pulse.

"You're wet," he crooned, sliding his hand around her, rubbing his thumb over her clit, pressing against her teasingly, circling around it with fast, sure strokes.

Then his hand was gone and she mewled in frustration, sliding her own hand down until she could play with her clit, circling around it and rocking her hips against her touch. His cock jerked within her and Rafe laughed that low, masculine sound a man only makes when it involves sex.

A thick, wet finger pressed against her anus again and she sobbed out his name as it slid inside, past the tight muscle, pushing in, in, in…until his finger was seated completely inside her.

"I'm going to fuck this ass again, and soon. I'm going to fuck your pussy, your ass, your mouth until no part of your body remains untouched by me. I'm going to mark you, brand you, so you know you're *mine* and if you ever leave me again…"

His other hand left her hip while he continued to pound inside her, his cock filling her pussy, his finger filling her ass. She screamed as he slapped at her ass, once, twice, and again, until the skin of her ass was on fire and hot little licks of hunger flooded her senses.

Sheila whimpered and pushed against him, rocking her hips, lifting herself for him. His hand struck her flesh again and Sheila shuddered, unable to even scream as her throat went tight.

He plunged inside her, withdrew, slapped her ass.

Her legs quivered against the side of the bed, the muscles giving out until she completely collapsed against the bed, unable to support her own weight any longer. His finger, the one fucking her ass, rotated within the tight confines of her anal sheath.

Then he slapped her ass again, his voice low and guttural as he murmured, "You won't leave me again. Say it."

She just shook her head, unable to find the words to speak. His palm came down on her ass again, the flesh hot, sensitized by the many strikes of his hand. His finger left her ass and Sheila whimpered as he withdrew. He kept one hand braced on her spine when she tried to lift her head up, when she tried to push back against him. "Damn it, Rafe, please!"

She could see him, just barely. The spit in her mouth dried as she saw his hand closed around his cock, stroking it quick and rough. One hand came back to her ass, spreading the cheeks and exposing her.

He came then, his seed cool and wet, coating her anus. When she felt him probing against her, Sheila stiffened instinctively, her hands clutching at the comforter. "Rafe…"

With just his semen coating her ass, he pushed inside, his voice a rough, threatening growl. "Say it. Say you won't leave me," he ordered, pushing deeper.

"Damn it, Rafe!" she hissed as he pulled out and started to surge inside her.

The tight ring of muscle relaxed just a little as she pushed down against him, arching her back as hot little streaks of pain started to bite at her flesh while he fucked his way inside the unprepared muscles of her ass. His hand came up and she tensed automatically as he spanked her, but the pain was a sweet, delicious little burn that had her rocking back against him.

The muscles in her ass, still locked so tight around his intruding flesh, relaxed slowly, so slowly, she never even realized it until he pounded against her, each deep stroke pushing her closer and closer to the edge.

She screamed as he slapped her ass again, circling her fingers desperately around the aching knot of her clit. "Say it, say it, say it!" he rasped each time he shafted her.

She plunged two fingers inside her pussy and started to come. One last hard dig of his cock pushed her over the edge.

"I won't leave," she gasped, rocking desperately against him, lifting her ass for him and whimpering as he responded with another burning hot lash of his palm against her flesh. "I won't…I won't… Rafe!"

She rode the climax, rode him, as it took them both flying, darkness clouding her vision. He was still slamming into her as she drifted back down, eyelids heavy, her lips still moving soundlessly, *I won't…I won't…*

He came in a rush, so hot, so scalding that it stole the breath from his lungs. His cock jerked inside her tight, silken little ass and he groaned, falling forward to collapse against her.

Her body was still quivering, but he caught sight of her closed eyes before he rolled to the side, the tissues of her ass clinging to him as his dick pulled out.

"Belle…" he murmured, pressing his lips against her back.

His only answer was a deep sighing breath. A slow smile curved his lips. He'd fucked her into oblivion.

Exhaustion dragged at him. His lids started to flutter down, but one of the curtained windows caught his gaze. "Shit…"

He stumbled from the bed, out into the hall. Throwing open the door in front of him, he saw the narrow twin mattress on the bed frame and muttered, "Good enough."

Gripping it, he lifted it but he was so damned drained, by the day, by Sheila, that his muscles quivered. He tossed it on the floor out in the hall and pulled the door closed tight, checking around him. No sunlight could reach here…he moved back into the room where Sheila dozed on, and snickered when his legs wobbled a little.

Closing the gleaming gold of the comforter around her, he lifted her and carried her out to the mattress, lowering her carefully before he collapsed beside her. He tugged the blanket until it wasn't trapped beneath her body anymore and snuggled up against her. With a sigh, he buried his face against her golden curls and let the darkness pull him under.

Epilogue

Leandra snarled at the note in her hand.

In broad, sweeping strokes, Mal had written, *Gone to Eli's. Meet me there.*

Eli's… Her mind spun back in time as she recalled the last time she had stood within that house.

Go on, witch, I won't ask for your life…

Clenching her jaw, she closed her eyes and threw her arms out. *Malachi, you ass,* she thought heatedly as she stepped into the void and let her magick carry her to Eli's house.

Alighting on the porch, she stared at the door and pounded on it.

Maybe he won't be here. Maybe he's Hunting…or on vacation.

Hunters *did* take breaks, she was pretty sure.

The door swung open and she scowled up into Malachi's face, not the least bit surprised that he'd opened it.

Stomping past him, she whirled around and glared at him, the thick locks of her braids swinging around with the movement before settling back around her shoulders. "Why do I need t' come here?" she demanded.

Mal smiled lazily. "Because I'm here. And I'm your trainer."

Lifting her chin, she said, "I don't like being here."

Malachi's smile changed, going from lazy and feline, to sharp and wolfish. "And why is that…"

His eyes moved over her shoulder and she turned slowly, watching as Mike came sauntering down the stairs. His eyes met hers and he stilled for a second, then his eyes went blank and flat before he continued on down the stairs and moved into the living room, leaving Leandra and Mal alone in the foyer.

Shaken, hungry, *scared*, she turned back and met Mal's eyes helplessly.

"Hmmm…I see," he whispered, the sound low, silken, wrapping around her, almost smothering her in its warmth.

And Malachi started to laugh.

Enjoy this excerpt from
Ben and Shadoe
© Copyright Shiloh Walker, 2005

Damn it.

This could be a problem.

He was here to protect her, to warn her, to teach her. And considering she had been living with her head in the sand for more than twenty years, that wasn't going to be an easy task. Being attracted to her was going to make it even more difficult—but if he felt the wolf inside him, felt the call of hers...

There was no if.

She was an Inherent born, if not yet changed. And he was a very gifted Inherent, a Hunter to the Council, and one of the few who had a touch of witchery through his mother's side of the family. He was a powerful witch, and that was how he had found her, but he suspected what he had in his veins was nothing compared to what lay untapped inside the woman in front of him.

Jillian had more than a touch.

Her mother had gifted her with such powerful witchcraft that it was amazing the earth didn't tremble as she walked. That a powerful, evil, dark seeker hadn't found her and tried to subjugate her.

Amazing that he had found her first, and was thinking that their powers and magicks wouldn't call to the other?

There was no if.

Stop it, Ben. We don't even know if she has the abilities, he told himself, shaking his head. He could smell something other than human on her, but that didn't mean she was an Inherent like her father had been. And the magick he smelled on her didn't mean she was a witch like her mother had been. She had gone more than a decade past the time when she should have first shifted. And no witch could ignore the call of magick for more than twenty years. Just because some old witch saw her thirty years ago, years before her birth, and said she would come in time to help fight some unknown war…

Visions were always subject to change. And maybe it was another Inherent.

Hell, if she was a witch, an Inherent, she would have changed when that werewolf attacked her five years ago. If she had…and if she had still been sentenced to jail…

And damn it, it had been Agnes Milcher who'd had the vision. Agnes…

Even as solitary as Benjamin was, he had heard of her. Her name evoked the same feeling that the vampire Malachi's did.

Shaking his head, he muttered, "Stop creating trouble where there is none. Wait and see what happens. See if she truly is gifted before you start planning."

He was also trying to fool himself.

Oh, she was a witch all right.

And an Inherent.

But somehow she had kept herself from changing.

Somehow she had suppressed her magick.

Or somebody had done it for her. From beyond the grave, perhaps?

For years.

She was the daughter of Carrick Wallace, one of Declan O'Reilly's father's right hand men. He and Adrienne had been murdered and their young daughter had gone missing twenty-three years ago. After Declan had walked away so many years before, the pack had reformed, restructured, and had executed the rogues.

They had searched high and low for Shadoe Wallace, the young babe mourned by so many.

And that child was Jillian, the woman who had fought off two rogue shape-shifters, a werewolf and an Inherent, and killed one of them.

She had done time in jail for protecting herself when she should have been coddled and praised, loved, adored, worshipped—shit, it made him furious just thinking of it. If he had found her just a little sooner, none of it would have happened.

Hell, maybe he was wrong. Maybe she wasn't an Inherent in truth. How could she have resisted the call of the moon, the call of the hunt, the magick of feeling the wolf's call for more than a decade?

She may not be a true shape-shifter, but she was more than human now.

He just had to figure out exactly what she was.

And soon. Before their enemies arrived.

* * * * *

"Ms. Morgan."

She went stiff.

Jillian knew that deep, almost growling voice. That voice had fueled a couple of very *interesting* dreams during the long, empty years in jail.

Benjamin Cross. Slowly she turned and met a pair of golden eyes across a distance of a few feet. She hadn't even considered that he would try approaching her. And now she realized just how foolish that had been. His persistence had known no bounds, so why had she suddenly expected that to change?

"I've no desire to speak with you, Mr. Cross. I do not give interviews," she said firmly, stifling the urge to stare as she gazed upon the man who had been calling her on a monthly basis for five years.

The phone calls had started within a month of her incarceration. At first, he'd just offered to come in and speak with her about her ordeal. Then he'd offered to 'interview' her for a book deal. Then he'd offered to interview her regarding her books. Although how he had discovered *that* piece of knowledge she didn't know. Then he'd just started calling to pester her.

Politely. Always politely.

But the phone calls never stopped.

A year into her sentence, letters had started coming, along with research books on magick and shape-shifters, and ghosts. The majority of her better books had in fact come from the man staring at her with those mesmerizing golden eyes.

Holy hell. It was a damn good thing she hadn't known what he looked like, otherwise she just might have given in to those interviews. Just for writer's curiosity, mind you…but *damn*.

His dark brown hair fell into his eyes in loose waves and he absently brushed it back with a lean, tanned hand, cocking his head and studying her intently. "You didn't really think I would just up and leave you alone, did you?" he asked, curiously.

She had the odd impression of a pup staring at her with his ears pricked. Or a wolf…shaking her head, she focused on a point just beyond his shoulder and said, "Actually I hadn't thought of it." Her eyes cut back to him as she added, "Or you."

"Ouch," he said mildly, those amazing brown eyes dancing with humor.

Of course, if she had known what he looked like...*oh, that would have been torture in there,* she thought helplessly.

Underneath the green chamois shirt he wore, there was a ribbed undershirt that stretched across his wide chest, his skin gleaming gold, muscles clearly evident beneath the clinging fabric. Worn jeans clung to his lean hips and long, muscled thighs as Jillian cursed her peripheral vision and forced herself to meet his eyes.

They looked...hot, hungry... A smell assaulted her senses, the smell of lust and the primal need to mate. Though how she could place such a name to that hot musky scent, she didn't know. Any more than she could figure out how she could smell it so clearly.

Hell, his eyes—gleaming, glowing...the striations in his eyes were starting to swirl and shift...

Unbeknownst to her, a soft whimper escaped her as she stared hypnotized into those eyes. She had seen eyes like that once upon a time and fear arced through her. A gasp fell from her lips and she retreated, her eyes wide and unblinking on his face.

And as she watched, the look left his eyes, his lids drooped, the odd tension seemed to leave him, and a gentle smile curved his mouth, the full lower lip curving just slightly. "I'm no threat to *you,* Jillian Morgan," he said softly, his voice intense. "To those who threaten you, I bring death—slow and painful—but I am no threat to you, ever."

He turned and left.

About the author:

They always say to tell a little about yourself! I was born in Kentucky and have been reading avidly since I was six. At twelve, I discovered how much fun it was to write when I took a book that didn't end the way it should have ended, and I rewrote it. I've been writing since then.

About me now...hmm... I've been married since I was 19 to my high school sweetheart and we live in the midwest. Recently I made the plunge and turned to writing full-time and am looking for a part-time job so I can devote more time to my family—two adorable children who are growing way too fast, and my husband who doesn't see enough of me...

Shiloh welcomes mail from readers. You can write to her c/o Ellora's Cave Publishing at 1056 Home Avenue, Akron OH 44310-3502.

Why an electronic book?

We live in the Information Age—an exciting time in the history of human civilization in which technology rules supreme and continues to progress in leaps and bounds every minute of every hour of every day. For a multitude of reasons, more and more avid literary fans are opting to purchase e-books instead of paperbacks. The question to those not yet initiated to the world of electronic reading is simply: *why?*

1. *Price.* An electronic title at Ellora's Cave Publishing and Cerridwen Press runs anywhere from 40-75% less than the cover price of the <u>exact same title</u> in paperback format. Why? Cold mathematics. It is less expensive to publish an e-book than it is to publish a paperback, so the savings are passed along to the consumer.

2. *Space.* Running out of room to house your paperback books? That is one worry you will never have with electronic novels. For a low one-time cost, you can purchase a handheld computer designed specifically for e-reading purposes. Many e-readers are larger than the average handheld, giving you plenty of screen room. Better yet, hundreds of titles can be stored within your new library—a single microchip. (Please note that Ellora's Cave and Cerridwen Press does not endorse any specific brands. You can check our website at www.ellorascave.com or

www.cerridwenpress.com for customer recommendations we make available to new consumers.)

3. *Mobility.* Because your new library now consists of only a microchip, your entire cache of books can be taken with you wherever you go.

4. *Personal preferences are accounted for.* Are the words you are currently reading too small? Too large? Too...**ANNOYING**? Paperback books cannot be modified according to personal preferences, but e-books can.

5. *Instant gratification.* Is it the middle of the night and all the bookstores are closed? Are you tired of waiting days—sometimes weeks—for online and offline bookstores to ship the novels you bought? Ellora's Cave Publishing sells instantaneous downloads 24 hours a day, 7 days a week, 365 days a year. Our e-book delivery system is 100% automated, meaning your order is filled as soon as you pay for it.

Those are a few of the top reasons why electronic novels are displacing paperbacks for many an avid reader. As always, Ellora's Cave and Cerridwen Press welcomes your questions and comments. We invite you to email us at service@ellorascave.com, service@cerridwenpress.com or write to us directly at: 1056 Home Ave. Akron OH 44310-3502.

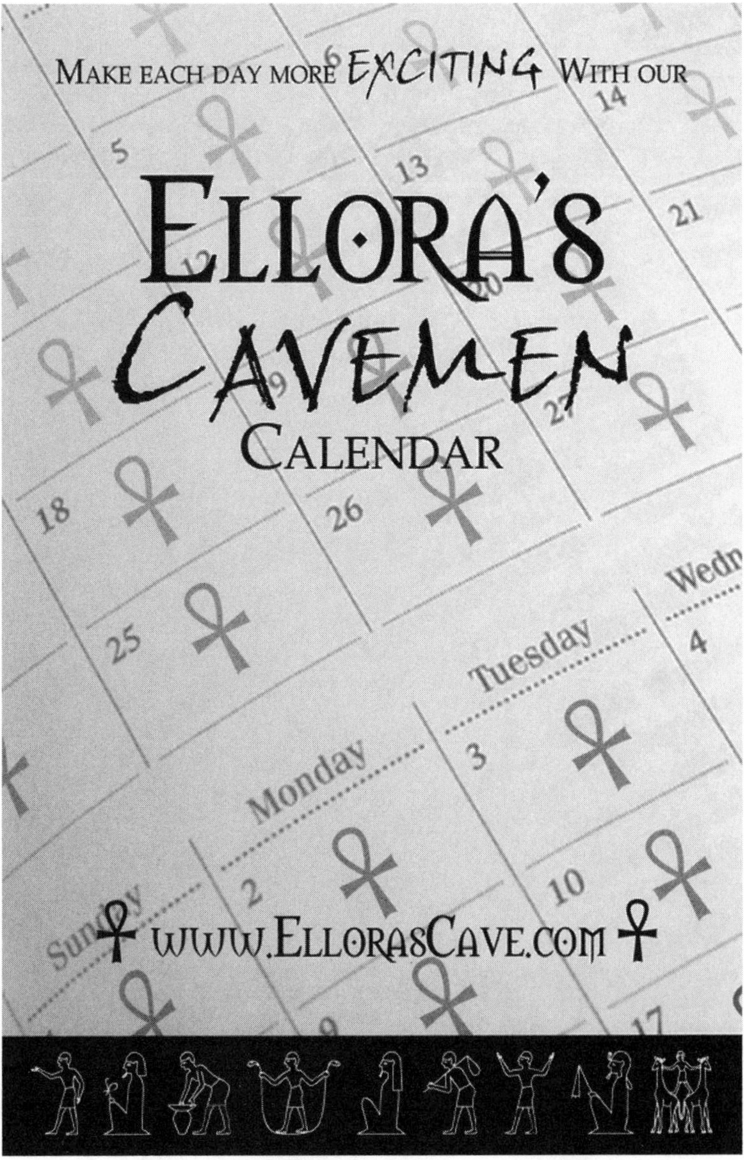
Make each day more EXCITING with our
Ellora's
Cavemen
Calendar
www.EllorasCave.com

Cerridwen, the Celtic Goddess of wisdom, was the muse who brought inspiration to storytellers and those in the creative arts. Cerridwen Press encompasses the best and most innovative stories in all genres of today's fiction. Visit our site and discover the newest titles by talented authors who still get inspired - much like the ancient storytellers did, once upon a time.

Discover for yourself why readers can't get enough of the multiple award-winning publisher Ellora's Cave. Whether you prefer e-books or paperbacks, be sure to visit EC on the web at www.ellorascave.com for an erotic reading experience that will leave you breathless.

www.ellorascave.com